READING GROUP CHOICES

2012

*Selections for lively
book discussions*

Prospect Heights Public Library
12 N. Elm Street
Prospect Heights, IL 60070
www.phpl.info

Published in the United States by Reading Group Choices,
a division of Connxsys LLC

ISBN 978-0-9759742-7-8

For further information, contact:
Barbara Drummond Mead
Reading Group Choices
532 Cross Creek Court
Chester, MD 21619
Toll-free: 1-866-643-6883
info@ReadingGroupChoices.com
ReadingGroupChoices.com

welcome to

READING GROUP *Choices*

Reading groups have discussed books and shared their joy of reading for years, if not centuries. They were so ahead of their time!

But now, it seems that many more people are getting it—books are becoming more social through the use of social networking sites, online book discussions, and eBooks with social-networking enhancements. Just as reading groups have done for so long, new technologies are helping to enhance the reading experience, to increase learning and to share the excitement of reading with friends, colleagues and even new acquaintances. The use of these new technologies in concert with printed books is reaffirming book clubs' passion for shared reading.

By bringing together diverse minds to discuss books and reflect on the ideas writers put forth, reading groups are continuing to broaden members' perspectives and to expand their knowledge, often causing groups' participants to re-evaluate their assumptions and even consider new philosophies and ways of living.

We hope this selection of discussible book suggestions will do all of that and more for you and your group!

—BARBARA DRUMMOND MEAD

Follow @ReadingGChoices on Twitter.
Become a fan of Reading Group Choices on Facebook®.

Book Group Favorites

Early in 2011, we asked thousands of book groups to tell us what books they read and discussed during the previous year that they enjoyed most. The top ten titles were:

1. **The Help** by Kathryn Stockett (Berkley Trade)
2. **Cutting for Stone** by Abraham Verghese (Vintage)
3. **Sarah's Key** by Tatiana de Rosnay (St. Martin's Griffin)
4. **Still Alice** by Lisa Genova (Gallery)
5. **The Book Thief** by Markus Zusak (Knopf Books for Young Readers)
6. **The Guernsey Literary and Potato Peel Pie Society** by Mary Ann Shaffer and Annie Barrows (Dial Press Trade Paperbacks)
7. **Hotel on the Corner of Bitter and Sweet** by Jamie Ford (Ballantine Books)
8. **The Immortal Life of Henrietta Lacks** by Rebecca Skloot (Broadway Books)
9. **The Girl with the Dragon Tattoo** by Stieg Larsson (Vintage)
10. **Little Bee** by Chris Cleave (Simon & Schuster)

Contents

The Beach Trees

By Karen White

From the time she was twelve, Julie Holt knew what a random tragedy can do to a family. At that tender age, her little sister disappeared—never to be found. It was a loss that slowly eroded the family bonds she once relied on. As an adult with a prestigious job in the arts, Julie meets a struggling artist who reminds her so much of her sister, she can't help feeling protective. It is a friendship that begins a long and painful process of healing for Julie, leading her to a house on the Gulf Coast, ravaged by hurricane Katrina, and to stories of family that take her deep into the past.

"[White] describes the land and location of the story in marvelous detail. . . . [This is what] makes White one of the best new writers on the scene today." —The Huffington Post

"White creates a heartfelt story full of vibrant characters and emotions that leaves the reader satisfied yet hungry for more from this talented author." —*Booklist*

About the Author: **Karen White** is the *New York Times* bestselling author of many acclaimed novels. She lives in Georgia with her family.

May 2011 | Trade Paperback | Fiction | 432 pp | $15.00 | ISBN 9780451233073
New American Library | penguin.com | karen-white.com
Also available as: eBook and Audiobook

CONVERSATION STARTERS

1. Why do you think Monica willed everything, including Beau and her beloved beach home, to Julie—especially as she still had family living? What were her intentions and what was she trying to say? What are the repercussions for Julie?

2. How does Chelsea Holt's disappearance shape Julie's life? What emotions still haunt her, even after almost twenty years?

3. What significance does the portrait of Caroline Guidry with the alligator brooch hold to her family? Are the sentiments diverse? What clues does it hold within it?

4. Do Aimee's flashbacks fill us in with an objective history of the intertwined Guidry and Mercier families? What critical clues does Julie glean from them to advance her investigation?

5. How does the search into the past—and for loved ones including Caroline, Monica, Chelsea, and Aimee's mother—influence the trajectory of the characters' lives and their relationships to each other? How do secrets come to define and haunt the Guidrys?

6. What motivates Julie to dig through old case files and artifacts to connect the dots between the two families? Do you think she was foolish not to let sleeping dogs lie? Would you want to know the truth, especially if it was unsavory? How does she end up untangling the mystery?

7. Why do you think the residents of the Gulf continue to rebuild after numerous tragedies—most recently from Hurricanes Camille and Katrina, and the BP oil spill—on the same plots of land that remain highly vulnerable? What might tie them to this place?

8. How does Julie's life mirror that of Aimee's? Both assumed a form of guardianship—of Johnny, Beau—and both seek answers to the unexplained tragedies in their lives, but what sets them apart?

9. Do you think Aimee and Wes did the right thing in loving each other from afar, keeping their feelings secret to spare Gary's heart? What were the consequences?

10. What did you think happened to Caroline? And who did you think killed Aimee's mother? Were you shocked by the revelations? What kept the secrets airtight for so long?

11. What were Ray Von and Xavier Williams' roles in the scandalous events? Do you think Xavier did the right and necessary things? Do you think he was effective in shielding Aimee?

12. What do you think the next chapter at River Song holds for Julie, Trey, Beau, and the rest of the Guidry family?

Breakfast with Buddha

By Roland Merullo

When his sister tricks him into taking her guru on a trip to their childhood home, Otto Ringling, a confirmed skeptic, is not amused. Six days on the road with an enigmatic holy man who answers every question with a riddle is not what he'd planned. But in an effort to westernize his passenger—and amuse himself—he decides to show the monk some "American fun" along the way.

From a chocolate factory in Hershey to a bowling alley in South Bend, from a Cubs game at Wrigley field to his family farm near Bismarck, Otto is given the remarkable opportunity to see his world—and more importantly, his life—through someone else's eyes. Gradually, skepticism yields to amazement as he realizes that his companion might just be the real thing.

In Roland Merullo's masterful hands, Otto tells his story with all the wonder, bemusement, and wry humor of a man who unwittingly finds what he's missing in the most unexpected place.

"Enlightenment meets On the Road *in this witty, insightful novel."*
—***The Boston Globe***

*"Insightful, amusing, loving. . . . There are lovely moments of enlightenment that are not accompanied by angels with flaming swords; rather, there is that peaceful blue sphere that is available to all of us." —**The Seattle Times***

About the Author: **Roland Merullo** is the critically acclaimed author of seven books. Merullo grew up in Massachusetts. He graduated from Phillips Exeter Academy in Exeter, NH, in 1971, and Brown University in 1975, where he also earned a Master's in Russian Language and Literature the following year. Merullo served in the Peace Corps in Micronesia. He has been a writer in Residence at North Shore Community College and Miami Dade Colleges. He lives with his wife and two daughters in eastern Massachusetts.

2008 | Trade Paperback | Fiction | 336 pp | $13.95 | ISBN 9781565126169
Algonquin Books | algonquinbooks.com | rolandmerullo.com
Also available as: eBook and Audiobook

CONVERSATION STARTERS

1. How do the first scenes of Otto with his family set the stage for what happens in the rest of the novel?
2. Do you believe Cecelia changes over the course of the story, or do you think it's only Otto's opinion of her that changes? Share specific scenes that support your view.
3. Which events or remarks in the novel convince you that Rinpoche is a legitimate spiritual teacher? Were there situations where you doubted his authenticity?
4. Humor is often employed as a way of making us relate to a particular situation. How does the author use humor in this way? Are there particular passages that were especially funny to you? If so, why?
5. The book is partly about "meaning of life" issues, but it also has a lot to say about contemporary American society. What does Otto see and hear that makes him encouraged or discouraged about the state of American life?
6. Discuss the role landscape plays in the story.
7. Jeannie, Anthony, and Natasha are minor characters in the novel, but how do they serve to round out Otto's character? How do they influence your feelings about Cecelia and Rinpoche?
8. Amish country, the Hershey's factory, a bowling alley, a baseball game, taking an architectural tour of Chicago, playing miniature golf, swimming in a Minnesota lake, why do you suppose the author chose these kinds of activities? Discuss the purpose each activity serves in the story. What would the book have been like had these activities not been included?
9. When Otto comes across the metaphor of the piano-playing boy in Rinpoche's book, he says, "If I had been editing the book, I would have written in the manuscript margins, 'Work this,' meaning that the author should take the general idea and sharpen it, make it clearer to the reader" (page 174). Yet Otto can't get the plight of the piano-playing man out of his mind. Why do suppose that is? What aspect of the metaphor is unsettling to Otto? Do you find it unsettling? If so, why?
10. How would you characterize what Otto experiences after sitting with Rinpoche for two hours in silence (page 237)? Have you ever experienced the pleasure of a quiet mind? Was it similar or dissimilar to Otto's reaction?
11. Do you believe the ending of the novel was the best ending for this story? If the story were to continue, where should it go from here?

Breaking Night

A Memoir of Forgiveness, Survival, and My Journey from Homeless to Harvard

By Liz Murray

"Breaking Night" is urban slang for: staying up through the night, until the sun rises.

When Liz's mother died of AIDS, Liz decided to take control of her own destiny and go back to high school, often completing her assignments in the hallways and subway stations where she slept. Liz squeezed four years of high school into two, while homeless; won a *New York Times* scholarship; and made it into the Ivy League. *Breaking Night* is an unforgettable and beautifully written story of one young woman's indomitable spirit to survive and prevail, against all odds.

"From runaway to Harvard student, Murray tells an engaging, powerfully motivational story about turning her life around. . . . In this incredible story of true grit, Murray went from feeling like 'the world was filled with people who were repulsed by me' to learning to receive the bountiful generosity of strangers who truly cared." —**Publishers Weekly** (**starred review**)

"Breaking Night itself is full of heart, without a sliver of ice, and deeply moving." —**The New York Times Book Review** (**Editors' Choice**)

About the Author: **Liz Murray** completed high school and won a *New York Times* scholarship while homeless, and graduated from Harvard University in 2009. She has been awarded The White House Project Role Model Award, a Christopher Award, as well as the Chutzpah Award, which was given to Liz by Oprah Winfrey. Lifetime Television produced a film about Liz's life, Homeless to Harvard: The Liz Murray Story. Today, she travels the world to deliver motivational speeches and workshops to inspire others. Liz is the founder and director of Manifest Trainings, a New York–based company that empowers adults to create the results they want in their own lives.

May 2011 | Trade Paperback | Memoir | 352 pp | $14.99 | ISBN 9781401310592
Hyperion Books | hyperionbooks.com
Also available as: eBook and Audiobook

CONVERSATION STARTERS

1. The book begins with Liz Murray comparing herself—physically and otherwise—to her mother. In what ways are they alike? What specific instances of difference can you find? What do you think it was that allowed Liz to actualize her dreams in a way her mother couldn't?

2. What do you make of Liz's intense need, when young, to assist in keeping her parents safe?

3. Articulate the different identities and resulting roles that the two sisters—Lisa and Liz—develop when quite young. Do you agree with Liz's idea that Lisa's time with a loving family explains her distant relationship with Ma and Daddy? What do you make of Lisa's harsh attempts to motivate and encourage Liz to go to school, or her cruel, disconnected treatment of her? Do you agree with the therapist's theory that the sisters couldn't be close because they were in competition for scant resources? How does their relationship evolve?

4. Throughout the book Liz expresses self-blame regarding her troubled situations. Discuss this as a behavior in children. What purpose does it serve for them? What are the consequences for Liz as she matures?

5. Spending time with the Vasquez family began a desire in Liz to keep her home life a secret. What role, if any, does this developing ability to hide significant elements of her life play throughout her life? When does this deception seem important? In what ways might it be harmful?

6. Eventually, Liz begins to shift from wanting to be involved with her parents, to the point of keeping watch during their drug activity to wanting to escape from her life with them. What are the causes or changes in her that help explain this shift?

7. Talk about Liz's intense relationship with Carlos. In what ways was it valuable or important? In what ways was it similar to or different from her life with her parents?

8. Consider the different essential needs of Liz at different stages of her life. What was most important to her when she was a girl who didn't yet attend school? During elementary school? At St. Anne's? At Brick's? On the street with Sam? Once back in school, at Prep?

9. After hearing Liz's story, what do you think about the nature of human will? Why are some people able to overcome such hardships and create a successful life, while others never can? Consider the role and function of social services. Did the institution fail, or did Liz refuse to be helped? Why do you think Humanities Preparatory Academy was so much more successful helping Liz?

Bright and Distant Shores
By Dominic Smith

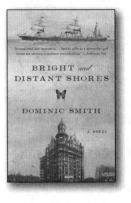

With critical praise lavished on his first two novels, Dominic Smith has become a celebrated and deeply revered storyteller. *Bright and Distant Shores*, his latest novel, offers a stunning exploration of late-nineteenth-century America and the tribal Pacific. It's an epic journey that fans of historical fiction will never forget.

In the waning years of the nineteenth century there was a hunger for tribal artifacts, spawning collecting voyages from museums and collectors around the globe. In 1897, one such collector, a Chicago insurance magnate, sponsors an expedition into the South Seas to commemorate the completion of his company's new skyscraper—the world's tallest building. The ship is to bring back an array of Melanesian weaponry and handicrafts, but also several natives related by blood.

Caught up in this scheme are two orphans—Owen Graves, an itinerant trader from Chicago's South Side who has recently proposed to the girl he must leave behind, and Argus Niu, a mission houseboy in the New Hebrides who longs to be reunited with his sister. At the cusp of the twentieth century, the expedition forces a collision course between the tribal and the civilized, between two young men plagued by their respective and haunting pasts.

"An absorbing exploration of culture, tradition, and renewal through the high seas adventure of three very different men." —Publishers Weekly, **starred review**

ABOUT THE AUTHOR: **Dominic Smith** grew up in Sydney, Australia, and now lives in Austin, Texas. He holds an MFA in writing from the Michener Center for Writers at the University of Texas at Austin. His short fiction has been nominated for a Pushcart Prize and appeared in numerous journals and magazines, including *The Atlantic Monthly*.

September 2011 | Trade Paperback | Fiction | 480 pp | $15.00 | ISBN 9781439198865
Washington Square Press | dominicsmith.net
Also available as: eBook

CONVERSATION STARTERS

1. Discuss Owen and Adelaide's relationship, and how it is affected by their different social and economic statuses. How are their views of each other influenced by each other's perception, rather than the reality of their feelings?

2. What are Owen's motivations for going on the voyage? What do you think influences him the most? Discuss Captain Terrapin's statement that "all men are equal at sea." (p. 129) Do you find this to be true?

3. Discuss the role of women in the novel. Think about Adelaide, her mother Margaret, and Malini. How do they exert influence over the men in their lives?

4. Among the Melanesian languages featured in the novel there is no future tense. What does this say about the Melanesian people? Who in this novel is living in the past, the present, or the future?

5. Why do Argus and Malini agree to act like savages and be put on display? Do you think they come to regret their choice? What do you think impacts Jethro's sanity? Is it the snake bite, or something else?

6. Malini thinks, "Weather and time; she was beginning to understand that these were two of the clayskin gods." (p. 354) Do you agree? Do you find that true in present day?

7. Why does Owen keep the effigy? He says, "It stood for all that waited beyond the brink. All that could arrive without invitation." (p. 434) What does he mean by this statement?

8. Reread Argus' thoughts as he confronts Jethro on page 456: "His sister, his island, his own boyhood self, they had all be defiled, each in their own way." Why does Argus react the way he does in this scene?

9. Death plays a large role in this novel. Contrast different characters' and different cultures' and social ranks' views of death, burial, and the afterlife.

10. The novel employs extensive foreshadowing. How is it used as a literary device? What major events did you notice were foreshadowed? How did this impact your reading?

11. Early in the book, the narrative is written from the perspectives of Owen and Argus, but later opens up to include limited perspectives from Adelaide, Malini, Jethro, and Hale. Is there anyone else you would have liked to hear more from? How did this contribute to the novel?

12. Discuss the customs and rituals presented in the novel, both of the native islanders and the Americans on the ship and in the city. What role does tradition and familial obligation play in the characters' lives?

Call Me Irresistible

By Susan Elizabeth Phillips

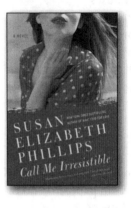

Call Me Irresistible is the book Phillips' readers have long awaited. Ted, the nine-year-old heartbreak kid from Phillips' first bestseller, *Fancy Pants*, and as the hunky new college graduate in *Lady Be Good*, is all grown up now—along with Lucy from *First Lady* and Meg from *What I Did for Love*. They're ready to take center stage in a saucy, funny, and highly addictive tale fans will love.

Lucy Jorik is the daughter of a former president of the United States. Meg Koranda is the offspring of legends.

One of them is about to marry Mr. Irresistible—Ted Beaudine—the favorite son of Wynette, Texas. The other is not happy about it and is determined to save her friend from a mess of heartache.

But even though Meg knows that breaking up her best friend's wedding is the right thing to do, no one else seems to agree. Faster than Lucy can say "I don't," Meg becomes the most hated woman in town—a town she's stuck in with a dead car, an empty wallet, and a very angry bridegroom. Broke, stranded, and without her famous parents at her back, Meg is sure she can survive on her own wits. What's the worst that can happen? Lose her heart to the one and only Mr. Irresistible? Not likely.

"Susan Elizabeth Phillips at her very best. Romantic, funny, sexy, and poignant. . . . If you're down or busy or distracted, I have the cure: Call Me Irresistible *is guaranteed to put a smile on your face."* —**Kristin Hannah**

About the Author: **Susan Elizabeth Phillips** is a *New York Times, Publishers Weekly*, and *USA Today* bestseller, whose books are published all over the world. Her first published work was written with a friend. She is married with two grown sons. Phillips currently lives in the Chicago area. Find Susan on Facebook.

August 2011 | Trade Paperback | Fiction | 416 pp | $13.99 | ISBN 9780062076168
William Morrow Paperbacks | harpercollins.com | susanephillips.com
Also available as: eBook and Audiobook

CONVERSATION STARTERS

1. What made Ted Beaudine so special—so irresistible? What kind of man do you find irresistible? Is it better to be in a long-term relationship with Mr. Irresistible or Mr. Regular Guy?

2. What draws Meg and Lucy together? Would you rather have Meg or Lucy as a best friend?

3. Are Meg and Ted ultimately a good match? If Lucy and Ted had gone through with their marriage, what might their lives have been like? Which makes the best match—a marriage of opposites or a marriage of similar personalities?

4. Most people envy those born to accomplished parents. Is there a dark side to being raised privileged? How did your family's economic status affect your upbringing?

5. Ted Beaudine is Wynette's hero and great hope, but being so beloved sometimes works against him. Can you identify in any way with the concept of the "burden of the beloved"?

6. Ted and Meg see Wynette differently. How would they each describe it? How big an impact does the place where you live have on you— your personality, relationship with others, world outlook?

7. At the Fourth of July party, Meg tells Ted she hates the town. He says, "Maybe. But you also like the challenge it's giving you." Has the place where you live or lived ever presented a particular challenge to you? Did you overcome it?

8. After years of traveling and searching, Meg finally found her passion. What makes her happy? What about Ted? Does everyone have to find his or her passion or is simply living well good enough?

9. Meg tells Sunny Skipjack, "Sometimes change is what we need. I guess it lets us look at our lives in a new way." Do her words reflect your personal experience?

The Doctor and the Diva

By Adrienne McDonnell

It is 1903. Dr. Ravell is a young Harvard-educated obstetrician with a growing reputation for helping couples conceive. He has treated women from all walks of Boston society, but when Ravell meets Erika—an opera singer whose beauty is surpassed only by her spellbinding voice—he knows their doctor-patient relationship will be like none he has ever had.

After struggling for years to become pregnant, Erika believes there is no hope. Her mind is made up: she will leave her prominent Bostonian husband to pursue her career in Italy, a plan both unconventional and risky. But becoming Ravell's patient will change her life in ways she never could have imagined.

Lush and stunningly realized, *The Doctor and the Diva* moves from snowy Boston to the jungles of Trinidad to the gilded balconies of Florence. This magnificent debut is a tale of passionate love affairs, dangerous decisions, and a woman's irreconcilable desires as she is forced to choose between the child she has always longed for and the opera career she cannot live without. Inspired by the author's family history, the novel is sensual, sexy, and heart-stopping in its bittersweet beauty.

"Classic storytelling and modern sensibility don't always come in the same package. But readers luck out with The Doctor and the Diva. *A book to treasure and recommend." —Bookpage*

ABOUT THE AUTHOR: **Adrienne McDonnell** has taught literature and fiction writing at the University of California, Berkeley. *The Doctor and the Diva* is based in part on the true story of her son's great-great grandmother. McDonnell was inspired by hundreds of pages of family letters and memories of elderly relatives, long haunted by the story. She lives near San Francisco. This is her first novel.

October 2011 | Trade Paperback | Fiction | 432 pp | $16.00 | ISBN 9780143119302
Penguin Books | penguin.com | adriennemcdonnell.com
Also available as: eBook and Audiobook

1. During the time the novel was set, it was assumed that a problem conceiving meant that the woman had fertility problems. Why do you think that was the case? Medically speaking, has that changed over time? What about with society as a whole?

2. Is it easier on a child to have a parent die or have a parent willfully abandon them? Why? Does Peter make the right choice in having Erika's father ask her to stop writing to her child? What are other ways he could have handled the situation?

3. Erika reflects, "If only I had been born without this voice. . . . It would have been simpler for everyone." (218) What does she mean by this? What if pregnancy and childbearing had affected the quality of her voice? Do you think she would have been happier? Why or why not?

4. Does becoming a parent mean that one must give up on dreams? How could Erika have had both a career and been a good mother?

5. It takes a long while after Erika arrives in Italy for her to send Ravell a letter. Why do you think she waits so long to get in touch with him?

6. Erika remarks of her accompanist and his lover, "Two men, friends of hers, in love. How very peculiar that was—contrary to nature's laws, for no child could ever be born to them." (283) In what ways is her statement hypocritical?

7. If Erika's first child had lived, how might things have unfolded differently?

8. When Ravell reveals that he was the child's father, Erika replies, "I guess I'm glad you did it." (387) Why do you think she says this?

9. Should Ravell have lost his practice due to his affair? Knowing that he helped so many couples conceive, could his indiscretion be overlooked? What about his actions in Erika's first pregnancy? Could his actions ever be justified?

10. Similar to the question above, if Erika had become a world–class opera star, bringing joy to millions, could she be forgiven for abandoning her child? What if she had left him to find a cure for cancer or some other humanitarian goal? Can a mother ever justifiably leave her child?

Don't Breathe a Word
By Jennifer McMahon

On a soft summer night in Vermont, twelve-year-old Lisa went into the woods behind her house and never came out again. Before she disappeared, she told her little brother, Sam, about a door that led to a magical place where she would meet the King of the Fairies and become his queen.

Fifteen years later, Phoebe is in love with Sam, a practical, sensible man who doesn't fear the dark and doesn't have bad dreams—who, in fact, helps Phoebe ignore her own. But suddenly the couple is faced with a series of eerie, unexplained occurrences that challenge Sam's hardheaded, realistic view of the world. As they question their reality, a terrible promise Sam made years ago is revealed—a promise that could destroy them all.

Jennifer McMahon returns with a vengeance with *Don't Breathe a Word*—an absolutely chilling and ingenious combination of psychological thriller, literary suspense, and paranormal page-turner that will enthrall a wildly diverse audience including

"[A] strange and unsettling shocker. . . . With the tale's outcome utterly unforeseeable even as it races along, Don't Breathe a Word *leaves you breathless."* —**Wall Street Journal**

"Beautifully written and spooky, Don't Breathe a Word *wraps around you and pulls you into a dark world of fairies and family secrets."* —**Chevy Stevens,** *New York Times* **bestselling author of** *Still Missing*

ABOUT THE AUTHOR: **Jennifer McMahon** is the author of *Dismantled*, the *New York Times* bestseller *Island of Lost Girls*, and the breakout debut novel *Promise Not to Tell*. McMahon grew up in Connecticut. She graduated with a BA from Goddard College in 1991 and then studied poetry for a year in the MFA in Writing Program at Vermont College. She lives in Vermont with her partner, Drea, and their daughter, Zella.

June 2011 | Trade Paperback | Fiction | 464 pp | $14.99 | ISBN 9780061689376
Harper Paperbacks | harpercollins.com | jennifer-mcmahon.com
Also available as: eBook and Audiobook

CONVERSATION STARTERS

1. Throughout the book, there are a lot of references to fairy tales. How do you think fairy tales mold children's perceptions about the world? In what ways do fairy tales represent or mimic real world problems and fears?

2. How do you think the Evie/Lisa relationship and the Phyllis/Hazel relationship parallel each other? Does one woman in each bond hold sway over the other? Is it always apparent who's really in control of the situation?

3. Throughout the book, it seems as if some men, or the idea of a man like Teilo, hold a strong power over the women. Why do you think this is? How are those men different from Sam and Dave?

4. Lisa's unwavering belief in the fairies, despite the skepticism of everyone around her, is a driving force in the story. Is a fierce belief in something a strength or a weakness?

5. At one point, Sam states that instead of having cancer and heart disease passed down in their family, they have malevolent stories. Do you think the stories we tell have the power to shape, even change, reality? Are there stories that have been passed down in your family that, true or not, have become part of how you see yourself and where you come from?

6. We get to know Sam and Evie both as children and as adults. How do you think their childhood selves compare to their grown-up selves? Do you think the adults they became were shaped by what happened the summer Lisa went missing?

7. Part of the book is told from the point of view of Sam's present-day girlfriend, Phoebe. She is the one character who was not part of the story's central mystery, Lisa's disappearance. Why do you think the author chose to tell the present day story from Phoebe's perspective? Is she an effective narrator?

8. From an early age, Phoebe has a complicated relationship with men and their place in her life. How do you think this affects her relationship with Sam? How do you think it affects her ability to trust?

9. Evie, in some ways, is the most complicated character in the book. She is fiercely loyal to Lisa, yet she betrays her terribly; she wants the truth to come out, yet participates in the deception. Does Evie truly have Lisa's best interests at heart? Is she responsible for all of her actions?

10. The ending of the book is open to different interpretations. What do you think really happened?

Dreams of Joy
By Lisa See

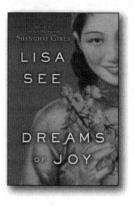

THE #1 *NEW YORK TIMES* BESTSELLER

Lisa See has brilliantly illuminated the potent bonds of mother love, romantic love, and love of country. Now, in her most powerful novel yet, she returns to these timeless themes, continuing the story of sisters Pearl and May from *Shanghai Girls*, and Pearl's strong-willed nineteen-year-old daughter, Joy.

Reeling from newly uncovered family secrets, and anger at her mother and hurt for keeping them from her, Joy runs away to Shanghai in early 1957 to find her birth father—the artist Z.G. Li, with whom both May and Pearl were once in love. Dazzled by him, and blinded by idealism and defiance, Joy throws herself into the New Society of Red China, heedless of the dangers in the communist regime. Devastated by Joy's flight and terrified for her safety, Pearl is determined to save her daughter, no matter the personal cost. From the crowded city to remote villages, Pearl confronts old demons and almost insurmountable challenges as she follows Joy, hoping for reconciliation. Yet even as Joy's and Pearl's separate journeys converge, one of the most tragic episodes in China's history threatens their very lives.

Lisa See, once again, renders a family challenged by tragedy and time, yet ultimately united by the resilience of love.

"One of those hard-to-put down-until-four in-the-morning books . . . With each new novel, Lisa See gets better and better." —Los Angeles Times

ABOUT THE AUTHOR: **Lisa See** is the *New York Times* bestselling author of *Peony in Love*, *Snow Flower* and the *Secret Fan*, *Flower Net* (an Edgar Award nominee), *The Interior*, and *Dragon Bones*, as well as the critically acclaimed memoir *On Gold Mountain*. The Organization of Chinese American Women named her the 2001 National Woman of the Year. She lives in Los Angeles, California.

May 2011 | Hardcover | Fiction | 368 pp | $26.00 | ISBN 9781400067121
Random House | randomhouse.com | lisasee.com
Also available as: eBook and Audiobook
Available in trade paperback February 2012

CONVERSATION STARTERS

1. Joy is frequently described in terms of her Tiger astrological sign. In *Dreams of Joy*, where do you see her acting true to her Tiger nature? Where do you see her acting un-Tiger like?

2. Does seeing the world through Joy's eyes help you to understand Pearl? Similarly, does Pearl give insights into her daughter?

3. The novel's title, *Dreams of Joy*, has many meanings. What does the phrase mean to the different characters in the novel, to Lisa, to the reader?

4. Although May plays a key role in *Dreams of Joy*, she is always off stage. How do you feel about this? Would you rather have May be an on-stage figure in this novel?

5. Pearl has some pretty strong views about motherhood. At one point she asks, "What tactic do we, as mothers, use with our children when we know they're going to make, or have already made, a terrible mistake? We accept blame." Later, she observes, "Like all mothers, I needed to hide my sadness, anger, and grief." Do you agree with her? Does her attitude about mothering change during the course of the novel?

6. Joy's initial perception of China is largely a projection of her youthful idealism. What are the key scenes that force her to adjust her beliefs and feelings in this regard?

7. Let's consider the men—whether present in the novel as living characters or not—for a moment. What influence do Sam, Z.G., Pearl's father, Dun, and Tao have on the story? How do they show men at their best and worst? Are any of these characters completely good—or bad?

8. *Dreams of Joy* is largely a novel about mothers and daughters, but it's also about fathers and daughters. How do Joy's feelings toward Sam and Z.G. change over the course of the novel? Does Pearl's attitude towards her father change in any way?

9. There are several moments in the novel when people have to choose the moral or ethical thing to do. Where are those places? What purpose do they play? And why do you think Lisa choose to write them?

10. Ultimately, *Dreams of Joy* is about "mother love"—the love Pearl feels for Joy, Joy feels for her mother, Joy experiences with the birth of her daughter, and the on-going struggle between Pearl and May over who is Joy's true mother. In what ways do secrets, disappointments, fear, and overwhelming love affect mother love in the story?

The Dry Grass of August

By Anna Jean (A.J.) Mayhew

On a scorching day in August 1954, thirteen-year-old Jubie Watts leaves Charlotte, North Carolina, with her family for a Florida vacation. Crammed into the Packard along with Jubie are her three siblings, her mother, and the family's black maid, Mary Luther. For as long as Jubie can remember, Mary has been there—cooking, cleaning, compensating for her father's rages and her mother's benign neglect, and loving Jubie unconditionally. Bright and curious, Jubie takes note of the anti-integration signs they pass, and of the racial tension that builds as they journey further south. But she could never have predicted the shocking turn their trip will take. Now, in the wake of tragedy, Jubie must confront her parents' failings and limitations, decide where her own convictions lie, and make the tumultuous leap to independence.

Infused with the intensity of a changing time, here is a story of hope, heartbreak, and the love and courage that can transform us—from child to adult, from wounded to indomitable.

"The Dry Grass of August is *a haunting debut about family bonds that stretch without breaking. . . . A beautiful book that fans of* The Help *will enjoy.*" —**Karen White, *New York Times* bestselling author**

ABOUT THE AUTHOR: **Anna Jean (A.J.) Mayhew**, a native of Charlotte, North Carolina, has never lived outside the state, although she often travels to Europe with her Swiss-born husband. Much of A.J.'s work reflects her vivid memories of growing up in the segregated South. A.J. has been a member of the same writing group since 1987, is a writer-in-residence at The Weymouth Center for the Arts & Humanities, and is a former member of the Board of Trustees of the North Carolina Writers' Network. *The Dry Grass of August* is her first novel.

April 2011 | Trade Paperback | Fiction | 352 pp | $15.00 | ISBN 9780758254092
Kensington Books | kensingtonbooks.com | ajmm.net
Also available as: eBook

CONVERSATION STARTERS

1. What do you think about Paula's decision to take Mary on the trip, given the antipathy in the deep south post *Brown v. Board*?

2. Why does Puddin so often try to hide or run away? What does her behavior say about the family?

3. Why didn't Paula try to stop Bill from beating Jubie?

4. Is Uncle Taylor a racist?

5. Why did the clown at Joyland by the Sea give Jubie a rose?

6. If you'd been Paula (or Bill) what would you have done when Cordelia failed to appear for dinner? How could they have handled that differently?

7. Why does Paula take Bill back after his affair with her brother's wife?

8. Did Bill and Paula act responsibly as parents when they allowed Jubie and Stell to go with Mary to the Daddy Grace parade in Charlotte? The tent meeting in Claxton?

9. Why didn't Paula punish Jubie for stealing the Packard to go to Mary's Funeral?

10. What drove Stamos to suicide?

11. Which major character changes the most? The least?

12. Which character in the book did you identify with the most? The least?

13. If you could interview Jubie, what would you ask her? What about Mary? Paula? Bill? Stell?

14. If Bill died at the end of the book, what would his obituary say if Paula wrote it? If Stell wrote it? If Jubie wrote it?

15. Given that there's little hope for Jubie and Leesum to be friends in 1954, what would it be like for them if they met again today?

Ellis Island

By Kate Kerrigan

Sweethearts since childhood, Ellie Hogan and her husband, John, are content on their farm in Ireland —until John, a soldier for the Irish Republican Army, receives an injury that leaves him unable to work. Forced to take drastic measures in order to survive, Ellie does what so many Irish women in the 1920s have done and sails across a vast ocean to New York City to work as a maid for a wealthy socialite.

Once there, Ellie is introduced to a world of opulence and sophistication, tempted by the allure of grand parties and fine clothes, money and mansions . . . and by the attentions of a charming suitor who can give her everything. Yet her heart remains with her husband back home. And now she faces the most difficult choice she will ever have to make: a new life in a new country full of hope and promise, or return to a life of cruel poverty . . . and love.

Ellis Island is both a poignant love story and a lyrical, evocative depiction of the immigrant experience in early 20th century America.

"Kerrigan is excellent at evoking both rustic Ireland and 20th-century New York." —**Publishers Weekly**

ABOUT THE AUTHOR: London-reared of Irish parents, **Kate Kerrigan** worked in London before moving to Ireland in 1990. She is the author of two books published in the UK, *Recipes for a Perfect Marriage* and *The Miracle of Grace*. She is now a full-time writer and lives in County Mayo, Ireland, with her husband and sons.

July 2011 | Trade Paperback | Fiction | 368 pp | $13.99 | ISBN 9780062071538
Harper Paperbacks | harpercollins.com | katekerrigan.ie
Also available as: eBook

CONVERSATION STARTERS

1. Ellie and John find a connection from the moment they meet and become childhood sweethearts. Do you think it is possible to sustain that relationship into adulthood? Are they truly soulmates?

2. What is Ellie's relationship with her parents? Is it understandable why she prefers spending time with John's parents, Maidy and Paud? What do they provide that Ellie's own parents can't?

3. How is early married life difficult for Ellie and John? When Ellie decides to go to America, John says that she's running away. Do you think there is some truth to this statement? Why or why not?

4. Isobel Adams treats Ellie not only as a maid, but sometimes as a confidant. Do you think this kind of behavior is appropriate? Is Isobel a good mistress and employer?

5. Seeing how happy her friend Sheila is with her fiancé, Ellie makes the observation that anything is possible in America. How is this true compared to what life was like in Ireland? Do you think this is true today?

6. Why does Ellie find Charles Irvington attractive? What can he offer her? If you were Ellie, who would you have chosen to be with, Charles or John, and why?

7. Why doesn't John want to move to America? Are you sympathetic with his views, or do you think he should have seriously considered Ellie's plan for him to join her in New York?

8. Do you think Ellie made the right decision in going back to Ireland? Why or why not? What would her life have been like if she had stayed in America?

9. What difficulties does Ellie encounter when she returns home? How does she use what she's learned in America to improve her situation there?

10. Ellie's story, which takes place in the 1920s, is a classic immigrant story. What are the similarities and differences with the immigrant stories of today? How about the immigrant stories in your own family?

Everything We Ever Wanted
By Sara Shepard

A recently widowed mother of two, Sylvie Bates-McAllister finds her life upended by a late-night phone call from the headmaster of the prestigious private school founded by her grandfather where her adopted son Scott teaches. Allegations of Scott's involvement in a hazing scandal cause a ripple effect, throwing the entire family into chaos. For Charles, Sylvie's biological son, it dredges up a ghost from the past who is suddenly painfully present. For his wife Joanna, it forces her to reevaluate everything she's hoped for in the golden Bates-McAllisters. And for Scott, it illuminates harsh truths about a world he has never truly felt himself a part of.

But for all the Bates-McAllisters, the call exposes a tangled web of secrets that ties the family together. The quest to unravel the truth takes the family on individual journeys across state lines, into hospitals, through the Pennsylvania woods, and face-to-face with the long-dormant question: *what if the life you always planned for and dreamed of isn't what you want after all?*

"Shepard delivers the perfect read. . . . A delicious story loaded with mysterious twists and turns and a vault of secrets, that when revealed, will keep you turning pages long into the night. Sara is a brilliant storyteller." —**Adriana Trigiani, bestselling author of *Very Valentine* and *Brava, Valentine***

About the Author: **Sara Shepard** graduated from New York University and has an MFA in creative writing from Brooklyn College. The author of the bestselling young adult books *Pretty Little Liars* and *The Lying Game*, as well as the adult novel *The Visibles*, she lives outside Philadelphia with her husband and dogs.

October 2011 | Trade Paperback | Fiction | 352 pp | $14.99 | ISBN 9780062080066
Harper Paperbacks | harpercollins.com | sarashepardbooks.com
Also available as: eBook

CONVERSATION STARTERS

1. Throughout *Everything We Ever Wanted*, Sylvie's house, Roderick, is as much a character in the novel as it is a setting. How do other homes in this story play a role? What is the significance of the empty houses on Spirit Street? Of Catherine's house in Maryland? Is it significant that Bronwyn and the members of Back to the Land don't have houses?

2. Both Sylvie and Joanna have complex relationships with their mothers. In what ways do these relationships affect the two women's choices throughout the novel? Are they seeking approval from their mothers, or are their decisions a form of rebellion?

3. Many of the tensions in the book are caused by what is left unsaid. Charles doesn't tell Joanna about Bronwyn, James never told Sylvie the details of the bracelet, and Scott doesn't volunteer any information about the wrestling team. How do you think this story might have turned out differently if the characters had been more open? What other instances in the novel can you think of where events are propelled by characters' withholding the truth?

4. James, Joanna, and Scott all feel disconnected from the looming shadow of the Bates family. How do their choices reflect this discomfort? Do you see this lack of acceptance by the Bates family as real, or are these three characters' insecurities largely of their own making?

5. This novel often seems built on the conflicts that arise from oppositions: wealthy versus middle class, the suburbs versus the city, adopted versus biological. What other oppositions can you think of? How are they significant to the story?

6. Much of the central drama revolves around Swithin, the elite school that Sylvie's grandfather rebuilt, even though all of the Bates-McAllisters have long since graduated. Why do you think the school still plays such a big role in the characters' lives? What is the significance of Sylvie's final decision regarding the Swithin board?

7. Sylvie's grandfather, Charlie Roderick Bates, is one of the most important figures in the Bates-McAllister family's life, yet no central character besides Sylvie ever knew him. In what ways does Charlie continue to influence the Bates-McAllister family?

8. On pages 208–209, Joanna tells Scott about her childhood excitement and eventual disappointment regarding the arrival of the Kimberton Fair. Why do you think Joanna shares this story? How would you relate this story to the rest of the novel?

Faithful Place
By Tana French

Back in 1985, Frank Mackey was nineteen, growing up poor in Dublin's inner city and living crammed into a small flat with his family on Faithful Place. But he had his sights set on a lot more. He and his girl Rosie Daly were all set to run away to London together, get married, get good jobs, break away from factory work and poverty and their old lives.

But on the winter night when they were supposed to leave, Rosie didn't show. Frank took it for granted that she'd dumped him. He never went home again. Neither did Rosie. Everyone thought she had gone to England on her own and was over there living a shiny new life. Then, twenty-two years later, Rosie's suitcase shows up behind a fireplace in a derelict house on Faithful Place, and Frank is going home whether he likes it or not.

Getting sucked in is a lot easier than getting out again. Frank finds himself straight back in the dark tangle of relationships he left behind. The cops working the case want him out of the way, in case loyalty to his family and community makes him a liability. Faithful Place wants him out because he's a detective now, and the Place has never liked cops. Frank just wants to find out what happened to Rosie and he's willing to do whatever it takes.

"French's emotionally searing third novel of the Dublin murder squad (after The Likeness*) shows the Irish author getting better with each book."*
—Publishers Weekly **(starred)**

About the Author: **Tana French** grew up in Ireland, Italy, the U.S., and Malawi, and has lived in Dublin since 1990. She trained as a professional actress at Trinity College, Dublin, and has worked in theatre, film and voiceover.

June 2011 | Trade Paperback | Fiction | 416 pp | $16.00 | ISBN 9780143119494
Penguin Books | penguin.com | tanafrench.com
Also available as: eBook and Audiobook

CONVERSATION STARTERS

1. How does religion appear to have influenced the families who live in Faithful Place? Why do you think Frank Mackey has rejected religion?
2. Why do you think that teenagers like Frank and Rosie—the ones who try to get away—appear to be the exception rather than the rule in the Mackeys' neighborhood?
3. Are Olivia and Jackie right or wrong to have taken Holly to visit Frank's family without his knowledge or consent? Why?
4. What meanings, ironic or otherwise, can be derived from the title *Faithful Place*? How do those meanings resonate through the novel?
5. Frank tells us early in the novel that he would die for his kid. Yet there are lesser things he chooses not to do, such as being civil to her mother and shielding her from having to testify in a murder trial. How well does Frank understand his feelings toward Holly? What are his blind spots where their relationship is concerned?
6. Why does Frank become so upset over Holly's infatuation with pseudo-celebrity Celia Bailey? Is his reaction pure, over-the-top exaggeration, or does he have a point?
7. Tana French makes extensive use of flashbacks to develop Rosie as a character and to flesh out Frank's motivations. How would the novel be different if it were narrated in a strictly chronological fashion?
8. Frank would appear to have every right to blame his family for much of the chaos in his life. To what extent, however, do you think his finger pointing is an evasion of responsibilities that he would be wiser to accept?
9. What feelings do the characters in the novel have regarding the decade of the eighties? How does growing up in the eighties seem to have affected Frank, his siblings, and his friends?
10. Does the Irish setting of *Faithful Place* contribute significantly to the telling of the story, or do you find that French's novel to be about humanity on a more universal level?
11. How does Frank's emotional involvement in the cases of Rosie's and Kevin's deaths affect his ability to function as a detective? Is it always a hindrance to him, or are there ways in which it improves and deepens his insights?
12. Near the end of *Faithful Place*, Frank and Olivia seem to have begun to move tentatively toward a reconciliation. What do you think is the likelihood of their succeeding, and why?

Falling Together
By Marisa de los Santos

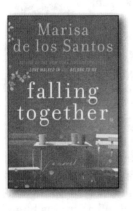

It's been six years since Pen Calloway watched her best friends walk out of her life. And through the birth of her daughter, the death of her father, and the vicissitudes of single motherhood, she has never stopped missing them.

Pen, Cat, and Will met on their first day of college and formed what seemed like a magical and lifelong bond, only to see their friendship break apart amid the realities of adulthood. When, after years of silence, Cat—the bewitching, charismatic center of their group—e-mails Pen and Will with an urgent request to meet at their college reunion, they can't refuse. But instead of a happy reconciliation, what awaits is a collision of past and present that sends Pen and Will, with Pen's five-year-old daughter and Cat's hostile husband in tow, on a journey across the world.

With her trademark wit, vivid prose, and gift for creating authentic, captivating characters, Marisa de los Santos returns with an emotionally resonant novel about our deepest human connections. As Pen and Will struggle to uncover the truth about Cat, they find more than they bargained for: startling truths about who they were before and who they are now. They must confront the reasons their friendship fell apart and discover how—and if—it can ever fall back together.

"It's the three-dimensional men, women, and children who populate her fiction that I'll remember for a very long time." —**Nancy Pearl's Picks**

"Her writing is both vividly descriptive and surprisingly insightful." —**Boston Globe**

About the Author: **Marisa de los Santos** is the bestselling author of *Love Walked In*, and an award-winning poet with a Ph.D. in literature and creative writing. She lives in Wilmington, Delaware, with her husband and children. You can find Marisa on Facebook.

October 2011 | Hardcover | Fiction | 368 pp | $25.99 | ISBN 9780061670879
William Morrow | harpercollins.com | marisadelossantos.com

CONVERSATION STARTERS

1. Describe Pen, Will, and Cat. What were they like as students and how has time changed who they are? All three of them have serious issues involving their fathers. Talk about how their relationships shaped their lives and their outlooks. Did you like any one character more than another? Why?

2. What drew Pen, Will, and Cat together, and what was it about each of them that created their magical bond? Why did they lose touch? Would they have come together eventually? What is it like when they are finally united? Would you go across the world to find an old friend?

3. What makes friendships work between people? Why is it often difficult to sustain friendships as we get older? How can we sustain them? Is it sometimes better to let a friendship die? Why? Have you ever enjoyed a friendship as special as that of the trio in the book? How did it begin? How did it impact your life? Can a person live without close friends?

4. Think about an old friend you haven't been in contact with for a while. What would you say in four sentences to describe your life in the time that has passed? Try it with members of your reading group. Think about what has happened since your last meeting and express it in a few sentences.

5. Pen has some interesting notions about love. She sees it as an "imperative." How does this view color how she sees love in her own life and in the lives of those around her—Will, Cat, Jason, Patrick, her mom? Would you say she's afraid of love?

6. Marisa de los Santos uses the image of falling in several ways throughout the novel. "There were people who could live on their own and be happy, and then there were people like Pen and Margaret who needed the falling together, the daily work of giving and taking and talk and touch." Discuss this example of falling. Identify others in the novel and explore how they relate to the characters.

7. Love, friendship, family, commitment, parenthood, loss, grief are many of the themes the novel touches upon. Choose one or two and trace how they are explored and resolved through the course of the story in an individual character's life.

8. While looking for Cat, Pen has her "jack-fish epiphany." Explain what insights she gleans, or as her colleague, Amelie describes it, "All is One and All is Different." Have you ever had a similar kind of "knowing moment" and when did it happen?

The First Day of the Rest of My Life
By Cathy Lamb

For decades, Madeline has lived in fear of her traumatic past becoming public. Now a reporter is reinvestigating the notorious crime that put Madeline's mother behind bars, threatening to destroy her elaborate façade. Only Madeline's sister, Annie, and their frail grandparents know about her childhood—but lately Madeline has reason to wonder if her grandparents also have a history they've been keeping from her.

As the demons of the past swirl around her, a childhood friend with a gentle heart is urging Madeline to have faith in him—and in herself. And as she allows her resistance to thaw, the pain she expects pales in comparison to the surprises headed straight to her door. With one bold, unprecedented move, Madeline O'Shea may just wake up out of the sadness and guilt that have kept her sleepwalking through life for so long—and discover that the worst thing that can happen is sometimes the very thing we desperately need.

"The complicated plot is surprisingly cogent, characters are well-drawn (particularly the grandparents), and extreme subjects like molestation and Jewish persecution during WWII are handled with a measure of sentiment." **—Publishers Weekly**

"The need to let go of one's past, instead of being defined by it, and to live in the present is good advice for just about anyone."—**RT Book Reviews**

About the Author: **Cathy Lamb**, the author of *Julia's Chocolates, The Last Time I Was Me,* and *Henry's Sisters,* lives in Oregon. She is married with three children. She writes late at night when it's just her and the moon and a few shooting stars.

July 2011 | Trade Paperback | Fiction | 480 pp | $15.00 | ISBN 9780758259387
Kensington Books | kensingtonbooks.com | cathylamb.net
Also available as: eBook

CONVERSATION STARTERS

1. Was Madeline an effective life coach? If you made an appointment for a life-coaching session, what do you think she would tell you to change? Improve? Or would she say that you have gathered your hellfire and are on the right course?

2. Alisha Heinbrenner, a client of Madeline's, says, "You know, Madeline. . . . I'm not lonely at all. It's bothered me that I'm not lonely, because I thought that I should be. But I'm not. Alone means I'm with myself. Alone means I answer to myself, I do what I want for, literally, the first time in my life. Alone means that I can think what I want. It means I'm not burdened with the constancy of doing things for others." Can you relate to this statement?

3. If you were on the jury at Marie Elise's trial, would you have found her guilty or not guilty for killing Sherwinn, Gavin, and Pauly? Did Marie Elise make the right choice? What would you have done?

4. In many ways, this was the story about a scratched and battered violin and the lives of the people who owned it over three generations. How did the author intertwine history, both during the Nazi occupation of France and back and forth to Madeline's childhood, to propel the story?

5. What did the lavender field symbolize? What did the swans and the Land of the Swans symbolize? The marbles? The emotional weather? Pink? The ice cream and pizza?

6. Was there a particular scene that best exemplified Emmanuelle and Anton's love for each other? Which one?

7. How did Madeline and Annie change from the beginning of the book to the end? Would they have changed if they hadn't been forced to change because of the article and the blackmail? What would they have lost if Madeline hadn't made her speech at the Rock Your Womanhood conference?

8. Madeline says, "I can only compare life to being shot from a cannon into the middle of space and being bombarded by all sorts of debris' pieces of satellites and shuttles, asteroids, shooting stars, maybe an alien spaceship. We're hit all the time and sometimes we can't find Earth. We can't even find the Milky Way galaxy. We're lost. Running around, dodging this and that, trying not to get hurt or killed, and all the while we're looking for home. That's how life is. It's a meteor shower." Is this true? What does it tell you about her?

Foreign Bodies
By Cynthia Ozick

Cynthia Ozick is one of America's literary treasures. For her sixth novel, she set herself a brilliant challenge: to retell the story of Henry James's *The Ambassadors*—the work he considered his best—but as a photographic negative, that is the plot is the same, the meaning is reversed. At the core of the story is Bea Nightingale, a fiftyish divorced schoolteacher whose life has been on hold during the many years since her brief marriage. When her estranged, difficult brother asks her to leave New York for Paris to retrieve a nephew she barely knows, she becomes entangled in the lives of her brother's family and even, after so long, her ex-husband. Every one of them is irrevocably changed by the events of just a few months in that fateful year.

Traveling from New York to Paris to Hollywood, aiding and abetting her nephew and niece while waging a war of letters with her brother, facing her ex-husband and finally shaking off his lingering sneers from decades past, Bea Nightingale is a newly liberated divorcee who inadvertently wreaks havoc on the very people she tries to help.

Foreign Bodies may be Cynthia Ozick's greatest and most virtuosic novel of all, as it transforms Henry James's prototype into a brilliant, utterly original, new American classic.

"Her vision of Europe and its tragic history is profound; and Lili is a creation of stunning depth. It is not Jamesian, it is Ozickian." —**Richard Eder, Boston Globe**

ABOUT THE AUTHOR: **Cynthia Ozick** is the author of numerous acclaimed works of fiction and nonfiction. She is a recipient of the National Book Critics Circle Award and was a finalist for the Pulitzer Prize and the Man Booker International Prize. Her stories have won four O. Henry first prizes.

November 2011 | Trade Paperback | Fiction | 272 pages | $14.95 | ISBN 97805475774
Mariner Books | hmhbooks.com
Also available as: eBook and Audiobook

CONVERSATION STARTERS

1. *Foreign Bodies* is described as a "photographic negative" of Henry James's classic novel *The Ambassadors*; in the *New York Times*, Charles McGrath described the similarities between the two books as "like someone pulling a glove inside-out." How does Ozick achieve this? And what do you think of re-writing a classic American novel?

2. Bea says about Julian, "A boy with a wife was a man, and a man with a wife could not be left to drown" (p. 81). How does Lili help make Julian a man? How does Lili's presence affect how Bea deals with Julian?

3. Lili's co-worker Kleinman reveals he's planning to move to Texas. How do the European characters view the United States? Are their ideas accurate?

4. Besides the trans-Atlantic divide, *Foreign Bodies* explores the transcontinental divide, specifically the differences between New York and California. Why did both Marvin Nachtigall and Leo Coopersmith leave New York for California?

5. A major theme in James's novel is the conflict between duty and personal desire. Where do you see this conflict arise in *Foreign Bodies*? Which characters are doing what they want to do, and which are doing what they think they should do? Who fares better?

6. Bea's role as "ambassador" is reluctant and ineffective, at first; she repeatedly fails to accomplish the tasks she undertakes for Marvin. But she is not powerless. Discuss the ways that Bea affects change in the book, in both her own life and in the lives of other characters. Are these changes always for the better?

7. What is the role of art in Bea's life? She married a musician at a young age; how did she see herself, and what were her ideas for her own life, when she met Leo Coopersmith? She told him she wanted to write a dictionary of clouds, a catalog of things impermanent and changeable; she said she wanted to make her mark. How did Bea's ideas for her life change? By the end of the book, have they changed again?

8. What role do the two grand pianos play in the book? When Iris taps one of the keys of the piano in Bea's apartment, what does she set in motion? That one note from Iris has its counterpart with another scene later in the book. What does that scene set into motion?

9. What do you make of the novel's last line: "Even so, in the long, long war with Leo, wasn't it Bea who'd won?" Do you think Bea won? Won what?

The Full Moon Bride

By Shobhan Bantwal

What makes a marriage—love or compatibility? Passion or pragmatism? Shobhan Bantwal's compelling new novel explores the fascinating subject of arranged marriage, as a young Indian-American woman navigates the gulf between desire and tradition. To Soorya Giri, arranged marriages have always seemed absurd. But while her career as an environmental lawyer has flourished, Soorya is still a virgin, living with her parents in suburban New Jersey. She wants to be married. And she is finally ready to do the unthinkable.

Soorya's first bridal viewings are as awkward as she anticipated. But then she's introduced to Roger Vadepalli. Self-possessed, intelligent, and charming, Roger is clearly interested in marriage and seems eager to clinch the deal. Attracted to Roger in spite of her mistrust, Soorya is also drawn into a flirtation with Lou, a widowed colleague who is far from her family's idea of an acceptable husband. In choosing between two very different men, Soorya must reconcile her burgeoning independence and her conservative background. And she must decide what matters most to her—not just in a husband, but in a family, a culture, and a life.

"Details of life as an Indian-American are vivid and telling." —RT Book Reviews

*"One of the best [novels] I've read this year. I couldn't put it down." —***Mary Monroe, *New York Times* bestselling author of *The Unexpected Son*

*"Compelling and memorable." —***Mary Jo Putney, *New York Times* bestselling author on *The Forbidden Daughter*

ABOUT THE AUTHOR: **Shobhan Bantwal** was born and raised in India and came to the United States as a young bride in an arranged marriage. She has published short fiction in literary magazines and articles in a number of publications. Writing plays in her mother tongue (Indian language—Konkani) and performing on stage at Indian-American conventions are some of her hobbies. She lives in New Jersey with her husband.

July 2011 | Trade Paperback | Fiction | 352 pp | $15.00 | ISBN 9780758258847
Kensington Books | kensingtonbooks.com | shobhanbantwal.com
Also available as: eBook

CONVERSATION STARTERS

1. Despite having a supportive family and a healthy childhood, why is Soorya Giri an unhappy woman?

2. After multiple rejections, Soorya finally meets a dream of a man, and yet she can't trust him. What are her reasons for such distrust?

3. What role does Soorya's father play in her life? Discuss the positives and negatives of having a parent who is neither good-looking nor charismatic and yet highly successful.

4. Are Roger's casual, laid-back ways merely a façade to cover up deeper personality issues?

5. Discuss Soorya's relationship with Lou Draper. What does Lou bring to her life and to the story? Discuss the pros and cons of a potential relationship between them.

6. Soorya's mother is a submissive and old-fashioned Indian woman. Is there a hidden core of steel within her? If so, how does it affect Soorya?

7. Discuss the conflicting effects of Indian and American cultures on Soorya's personal and professional life.

8. After admitting to herself that she's falling in love with Roger, Soorya continues to resist him and her own instincts. Why is she determined to keep him at arm's length?

9. Do any of the characters in the book remind you of someone you know? If yes, which character and in what way?

10. Discuss the role of Roger's family in the story. How does each member enhance the plot?

11. Originally the author titled this novel *A Twist of Karma*. Do you believe in fate and that everything happens for a reason? That Soorya and Roger were meant to be together?

12. As the family matriarch, what kind of impact does Pamma, the grandmother, have on Soorya's values?

The Gin and Chowder Club
By Nan Rossiter

The friendship between the Coleman and Shepherd families is as old and comfortable as the neighboring houses they occupy each summer on Cape Cod. Samuel and Sarah Coleman love those warm months by the water; the evenings spent on their porch, enjoying gin and tonics, good conversation and homemade clam chowder. Here they've watched their sons, Isaac and Asa, grow into fine young men, and watched, too, as Nate Shepherd, aching with grief at the loss of his first wife, finally found love again with the much younger Noelle.

But beyond the surface of these idyllic gatherings, the growing attraction between Noelle and handsome, college-bound Asa threatens to upend everything. In spite of her guilt and misgivings, Noelle is drawn into a reckless secret affair with far-reaching consequences. And over the course of one bittersweet, unforgettable summer, Asa will learn more than he ever expected about love—the joys and heartache it awakens in us, the lengths we'll go to keep it, and the countless ways it can change our lives forever.

"Nostalgic and tender . . . summons the passion of first love, the pain of first loss, and the unbreakable bonds of family that help us survive both."
—Marie Bostwick, *New York Times* bestselling author

About the Author: **Nan Rossiter** is the author-illustrator of several books for children, including *Rugby & Rosie*, an American Bookseller Pick of the Lists and winner of Nebraska's Golden Sower Award; *The Way Home*, one of *Smithsonian Magazine*'s Notable Books for Children; *Sugar on Snow*; and *The Fo'c'sle*. Nan lives in rural Connecticut with her husband, two handsome sons, and a yellow Labrador retriever named Mulligan. When she's not working, she enjoys hiking with her family . . . or curling up with a good book!

May 2011 | Trade Paperback | Fiction | 352 pp | $15.00 | ISBN 9780758246677
Kensington Books | kensingtonbooks.com | nanrossiter.com
Also available as: eBook

CONVERSATION STARTERS

1. From the very beginning the reader is aware that there is a strong physical attraction between Noelle and Asa. Are there any other (subconscious) factors that might have contributed to Noelle initiating an intimate relationship?

2. Asa has been raised to have a strong faith in God. He knows right from wrong and he struggles with the immorality of his desire for Noelle. Despite his faith and good conscience, he shamelessly betrays his father's best friend. How does this happen?

3. Noelle professes to love both Nate and Asa. Is it possible to truly love two people? Is it possible to be unfaithful to someone you truly love?

4. At what point do you think Nate suspects that the relationship between Noelle and Asa has become intimate? Do you think he is ever certain? Why doesn't he confront her?

5. Noelle struggles with overwhelming guilt and remorse. In her mind, how does she justify her actions?

6. What are some clues in the text that might lead the reader to surmise that Noah cannot be Nate's son?

7. After Noelle dies in childbirth, Asa turns his back on God. Is he angry with God or angry at himself? Is anyone to blame for the tragedy? Does God punish sin, or does He bless us in spite of sin?

8. Nate loves Noah and raises him as his own. Why does he do this? What does it say about his character?

9. At what point do you think Samuel and Sarah suspect that Noah is Asa's son? Can you imagine their conversation?

10. Asa sees Nate for the last time at Isaac's wedding reception. After seeing a picture of Noah, Asa tearfully excuses himself, but Nate stops him and says, "It's okay." What does he mean when he says this?

11. After reading Noelle's letter, do you think she was planning to leave Nate? If so, why did she go back home?

12. In the end, Asa discovers that he is already forgiven—and blessed! Do you think he will be a good father?

13. Are the lives of Asa and Noah—and Maddie—potential book material?

Girl in Translation

By Jean Kwok

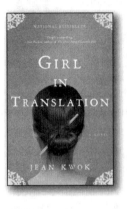

When Kimberly Chang and her mother emigrate from Hong Kong to Brooklyn squalor, she quickly begins a secret double life: exceptional schoolgirl during the day, Chinatown sweatshop worker in the evenings. Disguising the more difficult truths of her life—like the staggering degree of her poverty, the weight of her family's future resting on her shoulders, her secret love for a factory boy who shares none of her talent or ambition—Kimberly learns to constantly translate not just her language but herself, back and forth, between the worlds she straddles.

"It's hard to imagine a more winning character than the girl at the center of this deeply compelling novel. I can't wait for the next book from the very talented Jean Kwok." —**Ann Packer, author of *The Dive from Clausen's Pier***

"Though the plot may sound mundane—a Chinese girl and her mother immigrate to this country and succeed despite formidable odds—this coming-of-age tale is anything but. Whether Ah-Kim (or Kimberly, as she's called) is doing piecework on the factory floor with her mother, or suffering through a cold New York winter in a condemned, roach-infested apartment, or getting that acceptance letter from Yale, her story seems fresh and new." —***Entertainment Weekly***

ABOUT THE AUTHOR: **Jean Kwok** was born in Hong Kong and immigrated to Brooklyn as a young girl. Jean received her bachelor's degree from Harvard and completed an MFA in fiction at Columbia. She worked as an English teacher and translator at Leiden University in the Netherlands, and now writes full-time.

May 2011 | Trade Paperback | Fiction | 320 pp | $15.00 | ISBN 9781594485152
Riverhead Books | penguin.com | jeankwok.com
Also available as: eBook and Audiobook

CONVERSATION STARTERS

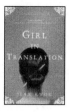

1. Throughout *Girl in Translation*, the author uses creative spelling to show Kimberly's mis-hearing and misunderstanding of English words. How does the language of the novel evolve as Kimberly grows and matures? Do you see a change in the respective roles that English and Chinese play in the narrative as it progresses?

2. The word translation figures prominently in the title of the novel, and learning to translate between her two languages is key to Kimberly's ability to thrive in her new life. Does she find herself translating back and forth in anything other than language? Can you cite instances where this occurs, and why they are significant to the story as a whole?

3. Kimberly has two love interests in the book. How are the relationships that Matt and Curt offer different? Why do you think she ultimately chooses one boy over the other? What does that choice say about her? Can you see a future for her with the other boy?

4. In many ways Kimberly takes over the position of head of household after her family moves to New York. Was this change in roles inevitable? How do you imagine Ma feels about it? In which ways does Ma still fulfill the role of mother?

5. Kimberly often refers to her father, and imagines how her life might have been different if he had lived. Do you think she is right?

6. Kimberly's friend Annette never seems to grasp the depths of Kimberly's poverty. What lesson does this experience teach Kimberly? Is Kimberly right to keep the details of her home life a secret?

7. Kimberly believes that devoting herself to school will allow her to free her family from poverty. Does school always live up to her expectations? Where do you think it fails her? How does it help her succeed? Can you imagine the same character without the academic talent? Must qualities like ambition, drive, hope, and optimism go hand in hand with book smarts?

8. Think about other immigrant stories. How is Kimberly's story universal? How is it unique? How does Kimberly's Chinese-American story compare to other immigrant stories? Would it change if she were from a different country or culture?

9. The story is set in the 1980s. Do you think immigrant experiences are much different today? What has changed? What has remained the same?

The Good Daughters
By Joyce Maynard

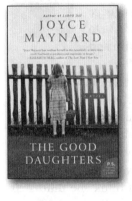

They were born on the same day, in the same small New Hampshire hospital, into families that could hardly have been less alike. Ruth Plank is an artist and a romantic with a rich, passionate, imaginative life. The last of five girls born to a gentle, caring farmer and his stolid wife, she yearns to soar beyond the confines of the land that has been her family's birthright for generations.

Dana Dickerson is a scientist and realist whose faith is firmly planted in the natural world. Raised by a pair of capricious drifters who waste their lives on failed dreams, she longs for stability and rootedness.

Different in nearly every way, Ruth and Dana share a need to make sense of who they are and to find their places in a world in which neither has ever truly felt she belonged. They also share a love for Dana's wild and beautiful older brother, Ray, who will leave an indelible mark on both their hearts.

Told in the alternating voices of Ruth and Dana, *The Good Daughters* follows these "birthday sisters" as they make their way from the 1950s to the present. Master storyteller, Joyce Maynard chronicles the unlikely ways the two women's lives parallel and intersect.

"Maynard offers fresh insight into what constitutes family." —**USA Today**

"Exquisite . . . . [A] beautifully written book." —**Publishers Weekly** **(starred review)**

About the Author: **Joyce Maynard** is the author of nine books of fiction and nonfiction, including the novel *To Die For* and the bestselling memoir, *At Home in the World*, Maynard makes her home in Mill Valley, California. Mother of three grown children, she spends her time in Mill Valley, California; in Lake Atitlan, Guatemala; and in various retreat centers with beautiful views, where, in addition to pursuing her own work, she runs writing workshops.

August 2010 | Trade Paperback | Fiction | 288 pp | $17.99 | ISBN 9780062015167
Harper Perennial | harpercollins.com | joycemaynard.com
Also available as: eBook and Audiobook

CONVERSATION STARTERS

1. The novel opens with a terrible storm. How does this beginning portend the events of the ensuing story?
2. Discuss Dana and Ruth. What is each like? What kind of households are they raised in? Each represents an opposing side of nature: one is scientific and practical, the other an artist and dreamer. How do their opposite personalities affect who they are and how they make their way in the world?
3. Both girls share a special relationship with Edwin Plank. In what ways are they similar in the eyes of this kind man one girl calls father and the other calls friend? What life lessons did they learn from him?
4. Think about Valerie Dickerson and Connie Plank. How did their personalities affect their views on family and childrearing? Analyze their relationships with their daughters. What did each girl share with these very different women?
5. Why didn't the adults correct the mistake that changed everyone's lives? Why didn't they tell the girls? How might events have been different if the girls had known what had happened? How did the girls' unawareness of the truth affect how they saw each other through childhood and beyond? Were the girls cheated in any way?
6. What made Dana's brother, Ray, so attractive to Ruth? Was it cruel to not tell Ruth the truth sooner?
7. What role did the Planks' farm play in the story? How are Dana and Ruth tied to the land when they are children? Does this change once they become adults?
8. When Ruth is living in Boston, Edwin comes to visit and they talk about her art and the nude models she draws. He says, "Back in my day, they made such a big deal about all of that, it made you a little crazy. If people could have talked about it and not acted like the whole thing was so sinful, maybe we wouldn't have gotten into so much trouble." What is Edwin referring to? Do you think he's correct?
9. After her breakup with Ray, Ruth forgave her father but not her mother. Why? What made her eventually forgive Connie?
10. Why didn't Ruth call Dana immediately when she discovered the truth about the past? Why didn't Dana tell Ruth after she'd figured it out? How did the truth set them free to be themselves?
11. What is the significance of the title *The Good Daughters*? How does it capture the story and its characters?

Great House

By Nicole Krauss

For twenty-five years, a reclusive American novelist has been writing at the desk she inherited from a young Chilean poet who disappeared at the hands of Pinochet's secret police; one day a girl claiming to be the poet's daughter arrives to take it away, sending the writer's life reeling. Across the ocean, in the leafy suburbs of London, a man caring for his dying wife discovers, among her papers, a lock of hair that unravels a terrible secret. In Jerusalem, an antiques dealer slowly reassembles his father's study, plundered by the Nazis in Budapest in 1944.

Connecting these stories is a desk of many drawers that exerts a power over those who possess it or have given it away. As the narrators of *Great House* make their confessions, the desk takes on more and more meaning, and comes finally to stand for all that has been taken from them, and all that binds them to what has disappeared. Nicole Krauss has written a soaring, powerful novel about memory struggling to create meaningful permanence in the face of inevitable loss.

"[Krauss] writes of her characters' despair with striking lucidity . . . an eloquent dramatization of the need to find that missing piece that will give life its meaning." —**Sam Sacks, *The Wall Street Journal***

ABOUT THE AUTHOR: **Nicole Krauss** is the author of two other books— *Man Walks Into a Room* and the international bestseller *The History of Love*. In 2010 *The New Yorker* named her one of the 20 best writers under 40. Her fiction has been published in *The New Yorker*, *Harper's*, *Esquire*, and *Best American Short Stories*, and her books have been translated into more than thirty-five languages. She lives in Brooklyn, New York.

Sign up for W. W. Norton's Reading Group Newsletter, e-mail readinggroup@wwnorton.com

September 2011 | Trade Paperback | Fiction | 289 pp | $14.95 | ISBN 9780393340648
W. W. Norton & Company | wwnorton.com | nicolekrauss.com
Also available as: eBook and Audiobook

CONVERSATION STARTERS

1. The large and imposing desk in the novel is passed from life to life, moving through space and time to link the characters in the novel to one another and to the past. What does this inheritance represent for each? Is it a burden?

2. A sense of loss—of a child, a parent, a lover, a home, youth, an illusion, and so many other things—suffuses the novel. How do the characters respond to loss, destruction, and change?

3. The novel is composed of intimate and emotional monologues that each have the tone of a confession. What do Nadia, or Arthur, or Aaron feel themselves to be guilty of? What role does judgment play in the novel?

4. Many of the characters are haunted by doubt or uncertainty, whether it's moral doubt, self-doubt, or the doubt that comes with a realization of the limits of how fully known we can ever be to one another, of how often we must live unknown and unknowing. What is the nature of Nadia's doubt, as expressed in the question that afflicts her: What if I had been wrong? What kind of uncertainty did Arthur feel in his marriage? And Aaron, as a father? What about Yoav and Leah Weisz?

5. Why do you think Lotte chose to give her child away? And why did Nadia choose to give up children, her marriage, a social life—everything but her solitude? What other kinds of sacrifices do the characters make?

6. What role does regret play in the novel?

7. What is the significance of the locked and empty desk drawer?

8. How does the story of Ben Zakkai and the destruction of Jerusalem—a response to catastrophic loss that led to a radical reinvention of Judaism that allowed it to survive in the Diaspora—relate to the rest of the novel?

Hotwire

By Alex Kava

Special Agent Maggie O'Dell, fresh from a grisly homicide investigation in the heart of a hurricane in coastal Florida, suddenly finds herself catapulted to the vast wilds of the Nebraska sandhills, ankle-deep in yet another mystifying crime scene. What started as a mischievous night of debauchery for a group of bored, local high school students has ended in a bizarre calamity, the teenagers attacked by an unidentified creature with the power to electrocute. As Maggie interviews the survivors for clues as to what really took place that terrifying night, local law-enforcement closes rank, making it clear that the seemingly harmless, rural landscape is home to some deeply buried secrets. Meanwhile, hundreds of miles away in Virginia, Army Colonel Benjamin Platt and his colleague, Roger Bix of the Centers for Disease Control and Prevention, are baffled by a virulent strain of bacteria felling whole high schools and elementary schools with a deadly form of food poisoning—and by the anonymous whistleblower leading them on a wild chase that lands them at a shady meat processing plant in Chicago.

The two investigations collide as a shocking web of government evasion and scientific experimentation worthy of the X-Files rises to the surface of each case. Lightning-paced and eerily prescient, *Hotwire* hums with intrigue, breathtaking revelations, and the trademark edge-of-your-seat storytelling.

"Twisted plots, shocking characters, breakneck pacing. Guaranteed to keep you up all night!" —**Lisa Gardner, author of Love You More**

About the Author: **Alex Kava**'s two stand-alone novels and seven novels featuring FBI profiler Maggie O'Dell have been published in more than twenty countries, appearing on the bestseller lists in the United States, Britain, Australia, Poland, Germany, and Italy. She is a member of Mystery Writers of America and International Thriller Writers. Alex divides her time between Omaha, Nebraska, and Pensacola, Florida.

March 2012 | Mass Market Paperback | Fiction | $7.99 | ISBN 97803074746051
Anchor | readinggroupcenter.com
Also available as: eBook and Audiobook

CONVERSATION STARTERS

1. Why does Maggie pocket Johnny Bosh's cell phone at the scene of his suicide? Is her action illegal? What information does the phone reveal about Amanda Vicks?
2. *Hotwire* tackles themes of domestic terrorism, bioengineering, genetically altered food, teenage drug use, bullying, government subterfuge, military misconduct and the dangers of the meat processing industry. How does the author maneuver these weighty topics so that they do not topple the narrative?
3. What prompts Lucy's comment to Maggie, "I think you and I were meant to be oddities no matter where we are or what we do"? Do you think Kava favors her female characters? Are there any male characters in the novel as fully developed and as principled as Lucy or Maggie?
4. What does Kava's skillful evocation of the Nebraska landscape—the rolling red and gold grasses of the sandhills, the eerie vastness of the man-made pine forest—add to this story?
5. Maggie has no jurisdiction to be lead investigator on the case of the injured and dead teens, yet she decides to stay in Nebraska long enough to make sure the investigation is handled properly. "But Maggie was here because she wanted—no, she needed—to see that Dawson Hayes was okay." Why does she feel so connected to Dawson, the self-proclaimed loser? Does this sense of connection persist?
6. Who follows Platt home from Williamsburg, and pays his parents a "friendly" visit as a warning to Platt to drop his investigation?
7. Maggie is obsessed with her boss's apparent scorn for her. What explains Kunze's suddenly magnanimous behavior at the end of the novel, when he gives Maggie the week off, with "no lecture, no punishment, no suspension," despite her going awol from her conference in Denver?
8. Do you read Wesley Stotter as a UFO-chasing eccentric, or as an earnest theorist who can't make himself heard? Does his sudden demise in the fieldhouse come as a surprise? What mystery is he on the verge of cracking at the moment of his death? Does the book supply an answer to this mystery?
9. In the novel's opening lines, Dawson Hayes muses that, for teenagers, "Admission to the cool club didn't come without some sacrifice." How is this adage applicable to many of the adults in the novel, as they wrangle for professional leverage?

I'd Know You Anywhere

By Laura Lippman

Suburban wife and mother Eliza Benedict's peaceful world falls off its axis when a letter arrives from Walter Bowman. In the summer of 1985, when Eliza was fifteen, she was kidnapped by this man and held hostage for almost six weeks. Now he's on death row in Virginia for the rape and murder of his final victim, and Eliza wants nothing to do with him. Walter, however, is unpredictable when ignored—as Eliza knows only too well—and to shelter her children from the nightmare of her past, she'll see him one last time.

But Walter is after something more than forgiveness: He wants Eliza to save his life . . . and he wants her to remember the truth about that long-ago summer and release the terrible secret she's keeping buried inside.

With *I'd Know You Anywhere*, Lippman tells a gripping and richly textured tale of a young woman whose life dangerously entwines once again with a man on Death Row who had kidnapped her when she was a teenager.

"The best suspense novel of the year." —**Stephen King**, *Entertainment Weekly*

"Laura Lippman is among the select group of novelists who have invigorated the crime fiction arena with smart, innovative, and exciting work."
—**George Pelecanos**

ABOUT THE AUTHOR: **Laura Lippman** grew up in Baltimore and returned to her hometown to work as a journalist. After writing seven books while still a full-time reporter, she left the *Baltimore Sun* to focus on fiction. She is the author of eleven Tess Monaghan books, including *Baltimore Blues* and *The Girl in the Green Raincoat*; five stand-alone novels, including *The Most Dangerous Thing* and *What the Dead Know*; and one short story collection. Lippman has won numerous awards for her work, including the Edgar, Quill, Anthony, Nero Wolfe, Agatha, Gumshoe, Barry, and Macavity and is a *New York Times* bestselling author. Find her on Facebook.

May 2011 | Trade Paperback | Fiction | 400 pp | $14.99 | ISBN 9780062070753
William Morrow Paperbacks | harpercollins.com | lauralippman.com
Also available as: eBook and Audiobook

1. Describe Eliza as an adult and as a teenager. What of her personality is the same? How did the trauma of her kidnapping impact her relationship with her family?

2. What did Eliza have in common with Walter's other victims? Why didn't Walter kill her too?

3. When she visits the parents of Walter's last victim, Eliza can't help but think of their daughter and her role—or lack of it—in her death. Discuss the questions Eliza raises about her own culpability. Does Eliza share any blame for Holly's death?

4. How did knowing Walter as intimately as she did save Eliza's life? Which person knew the other better? Did she owe Walter his life—or anything at all—since ultimately, he spared hers? Did he know her as well as he thought? Were you surprised by the outcome when she finally visited?

5. What does Walter want from Eliza? What does she want from him?

6. Eliza had felt protected by the invisibility with which she cloaked herself. Can we ever truly hide from those who want to find us? What is the emotional cost for Eliza?

7. Eliza wished her son could stay young and innocent for years. "But she knew there was no spell, no magic, that could keep a child a child, or shield a child from the world at large. In fact, that was where the trouble almost always began, with a parent trying to out-think fate." Why does Eliza think this way? What does she mean by "that was where the trouble almost always began"? Are we overprotective of our children?

8. When she was asked if Walter deserved to die, Eliza responds, "It doesn't matter what I think. He was sentenced for the murder of Holly Tackett, and her parents made it clear that they approved of the death penalty. I wasn't consulted." Do you think Walter deserved to die? Why is it so difficult for Eliza to offer her opinion? Do you think she feels guilty for surviving?

9. Eliza's sister Vonnie accuses her of "existing . . . You let life happen to you. You live the most reactive life of anyone I know. If there's one thing I would have learned from your experience, I think it would be to never let anyone else take control of my life." Is Vonnie correct in her assessment? Has Eliza learned this lesson?

The Immortal Life of Henrietta Lacks
By Rebecca Skloot

Her name was Henrietta Lacks, but scientists know her as HeLa. She was a poor black tobacco farmer whose cells—taken without her knowledge in 1951—became one of the most important tools in medicine, vital for developing the polio vaccine, cloning, gene mapping, in vitro fertilization, and more. Henrietta's cells have been bought and sold by the billions, yet she remains virtually unknown, and her family can't afford health insurance.

This *New York Times* bestseller takes readers on an extraordinary journey, from the "colored" ward of Johns Hopkins Hospital in the 1950s to stark white laboratories with freezers filled with HeLa cells, from Henrietta's small, dying hometown of Clover, Virginia, to East Baltimore today, where her children and grandchildren live and struggle with the legacy of her cells. It's a story inextricably connected to the dark history of experimentation on African Americans, the birth of bioethics, and the legal battles over whether we control the stuff we're made of.

"Science writing is often just about 'the facts.' Skloot's book, her first, is far deeper, braver, and more wonderful." —**New York Times Book Review**

ABOUT THE AUTHOR: **Rebecca Skloot** is an award-winning science writer. She is coeditor of *The Best American Science Writing 2011* and has worked as a correspondent for NPR and PBS. Skloot's debut book, *The Immortal Life of Henrietta Lacks,* took more than a decade to research and write. Skloot is the founder and president of The Henrietta Lacks Foundation. She has a B.S. in biological sciences and an MFA in creative nonfiction. She has taught creative writing and science journalism at the University of Memphis, the University of Pittsburgh, and New York University. She lives in Chicago.

March 2011 | Trade Paperback | Nonfiction | 400 pp | $16.00 | ISBN 9781400052189
Broadway Books | CrownPublishing.com | rebeccaskloot.com
Also available as: eBook and Audiobook

CONVERSATION STARTERS

1. On page xiii, Rebecca Skloot states, "This is a work of nonfiction. No names have been changed, no characters invented, no events fabricated." Consider the process Skloot went through to verify dialogue, re-create scenes, and establish facts.

2. In a review for the *New York Times*, Dwight Garner writes, "Ms. Skloot is a memorable character herself. She never intrudes on the narrative, but she takes us along with her on her reporting." How would the story have been different if she had not been a part of it?

3. Deborah shares her mother's medical records with Skloot but is adamant that she not copy everything. Deborah says, "Everybody in the world got her cells, only thing we got of our mother is just them records and her Bible." Discuss the deeper meaning behind this statement. If you were in Deborah's situation, how would you react to someone wanting to look into your mother's medical records?

4. As a journalist, Skloot is careful to present the encounter between the Lacks family and the world of medicine without taking sides. Since readers bring their own experiences and opinions to the text, some may feel she took the scientists' side, while others may feel she took the family's side. Does your opinion fall on one side or the other, and why?

5. Henrietta signed a consent form that said, "I hereby give consent to the staff of The Johns Hopkins Hospital to perform any operative procedures and under any anesthetic either local or general that they may deem necessary in the proper surgical care and treatment of: _____." Do you believe TeLinde and Gey had the right to obtain a sample from her cervix to use in their research? Do you think Henrietta would have given explicit consent to have a tissue sample used in medical research if she had been given all the information? Do you always thoroughly read consent forms?

6. Deborah says, "But I always have thought it was strange, if our mother cells done so much for medicine, how come her family can't afford to see no doctors?" Should the family be financially compensated for the HeLa cells? Do you feel the Lacks deserve health insurance even though they can't afford it? How would you respond if you were in their situation?

7. Reflect upon Henrietta's life: What challenges did she and her family face? What do you think their greatest strengths were? How did she face death? What do you think that says about the type of person she was?

Impatient With Desire

The Lost Journal of Tamsen Donner

By Gabrielle Burton

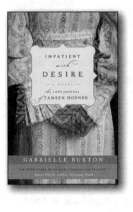

The extraordinary novel from award-winning author Gabrielle Burton captures the struggle of a historical heroine in her attempt to balance adventure, love, and family.

Tamsen Donner was a pioneer in 1846 in more ways than one. After months of preparation and research, she and her husband George, along with their five daughters and eighty other pioneers, headed west on the California-Oregon Trail in eager anticipation of new lives in California. But everything that could go wrong did . . . and an American legend was born.

The Donner Party. We may think we know their story—a cautionary tale of starving pioneers trapped in the mountains performing an unspeakable act to survive—but *Impatient with Desire* brings to stunning life a woman—and a love story—behind the myth.

In *Impatient with Desire*, Burton imagines Tamsen's famous lost journal, bringing to life a remarkable heroine in an extraordinary situation. A timeless American story written from a woman's perspective, NPR called this winner of the Western Heritage Award: "The literary equivalent of El Dorado—The Lost City of Gold."

"Burton's writing tears out the reader's heart as it brings closure to her quest to understand a woman lost to time. Impatient With Desire *finally rescues Tamsen Donner from ignominy, bringing her back to us a robust and very alive woman."* —**Erika Schikel, *Los Angeles Times***

About the Author: **Gabrielle Burton** is the author of *I'm Running Away from Home but I'm Not Allowed to Cross the Street, Heartbreak Hotel,* and the memoir, *Searching for Tamsen Donner.* Her prizes include the Maxwell Perkins Prize, the Great Lakes Colleges Association New Writers Award, the Nicholl Fellowship in screenwriting given by the Academy of Motion Picture Arts and Sciences, and the Mary Pickford prize for screenwriting. She lives in Venice, California.

March 2011 | Trade Paperback | Fiction | 256 pp | $13.99 | ISBN 9781401341664
Voice | hyperionbooks.com | gabrielleburton.com
Also available as: eBook

CONVERSATION STARTERS

1. *Impatient with Desire* begins with the following sentence: "Imagine all the roads a woman and a man walk until the reach the road they'll walk together." What multiple levels of meanings does this sentence have within the context of the novel? Why is the metaphor of a road an especially evocative first impression for *Impatient with Desire*?

2. Why do you think Burton chose to write this novel as a journal, from Tamsen's first person perspective? Were you sympathetic toward Tamsen or did you judge her decisions? Ultimately, did you admire Tamsen or not?

3. The concept of "desire" runs throughout the narrative—desire for food, for adventure, for freedom, for respect. On page 140, Tamsen stated: "Yet, every time I bid one of our Ohio-bound neighbors farewell, desire leapt in me. All my life, I have wondered about the place I'm not in. You either are that way or you aren't, and you can't imagine the opposite state." (140) Do you agree with Tamsen? Which state do you align with? Can you understand the other perspective?

4. We learn during the section titled "Hastings Cutoff" that if the women had been able to influence the route with their votes, the party may have never been stranded. Does Tamsen ever blame George for their predicament?

5. On page 77–78, Tamsen reflects, "I've lived years on farms, and know incontestably that the strong survive, the weak die off. That is the way of nature, but I used to argue that we can improve on nature, or at least not be as brutal as nature." After resorting to cannibalism to keep her children alive, Tamsen thinks: "And now the great violation is done once, twice, and as many more times as needed, and all I feel is deep relief that the children are visibly stronger and an equally deep anger." (205) As omnivores, humans are able to eat just about anything, but choose not to for moral and ethical reasons. Cannibalism is one of our greatest cultural taboos. However, what would you do to save your children?

6. On page 81, Tamsen writes to her sister, ". . . I find that, when I revisit the past, it often reveals something quite unexpected—too often some humbling or unpleasant truth that seems clear as day now." What does revisiting the Donner tragedy reveal to us as individuals as well as culturally?

7. What "life lesson" can be learned from Tamsen's story? What did you learn? About Tamsen Donner? About yourself?

I Remember Nothing

By Nora Ephron

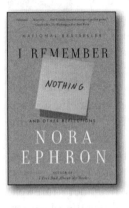

Nora Ephron returns with her first book since the astounding success of *I Feel Bad About My Neck*, taking a cool, hard, hilarious look at the past, the present, and the future, bemoaning the vicissitudes of modern life, and recalling with her signature clarity and wisdom everything she hasn't (yet) forgotten.

Ephron writes about falling hard for a way of life ("Journalism: A Love Story") and about breaking up even harder with the men in her life ("The D Word"); lists "Twenty-five Things People Have a Shocking Capacity to Be Surprised by Over and Over Again" ("There is no explaining the stock market but people try;" "You can never know the truth of anyone's marriage, including your own;" "Cary Grant was Jewish;" "Men cheat"); reveals the alarming evolution, a decade after she wrote and directed *You've Got Mail*, of her relationship with her in-box ("The Six Stages of E-Mail"); and asks the age-old question, which came first, the chicken soup or the cold? All the while, she gives candid, edgy voice to everything women who have reached a certain age have been thinking . . . but rarely acknowledging.

"Fabulous . . . Masterly . . . [Ephron is] a tremendously talented woman . . . She'll dazzle you with strings of perfect prose." —**Carolyn See, *The Washington Post Book World***

ABOUT THE AUTHOR: **Nora Ephron** is also the author *of I Feel Bad About My Neck, Crazy Salad, Scribble Scribble, Wallflower at the Orgy*, and *Heartburn*. She received Academy Award nominations for Best Original Screenplay for *When Harry Met Sally...*, *Silkwood*, and *Sleepless in Seattle*, which she also directed. Her other credits include the films *Michael, You've Got Mail*, and the play *Imaginary Friends*. She lives in New York City with her husband, writer Nicholas Pileggi.

November 2011 | Trade Paperback | Fiction | 160 pp | $14.00 | ISBN 9780307742803
Vintage | readinggroupcenter.com
Also available as: eBook and Audiobook

CONVERSATION STARTERS

1. In the title essay, Ephron writes, ". . . I have been forgetting things for years, but now I forget in a new way" (p. 5). How do the examples she uses capture the difference between her past and present ways of forgetting?

2. "The Legend" offers a colorful portrait of Ephron's childhood surrounded by Hollywood and literary celebrities, including her mother, a highly successful screenwriter, and the noted New Yorker writer, Lillian Ross. Discuss the various implications of the title. What does the anecdote at the heart of the essay, as well as the vignette about her graduation, convey about Ephron's feelings for her mother? How does she capture the ambivalence experienced by a child of an alcoholic?

3. "My Life as an Heiress" provides more glimpses into the dynamics of Ephron's family. How does she use humor and exaggeration to explore the relationships among her siblings—and the unexpected and less-than-admirable qualities triggered by the anticipation of an unexpected financial boom?

4. What does "Twenty-five Things People Have a Shocking Capacity to Be Surprised by Over and Over Again" reveal about human nature and our tendency to accept conventional beliefs despite lots of evidence to the contrary? What particular needs, emotions, or prejudices perpetuate our "capacity to be surprised"? Which entries resonated with you? What would you add to her list?

5. "The Six Stages of E-Mail" is a very funny chronicle of Ephron's evolving reactions to e-mail. Do you share her mixed feelings about e-mail and more recent (and, perhaps, more intrusive) technological advances like Facebook and other social networks? Have these new forms of communication made life easier or more complicated?

6. Ephron writes, "The realization that I may only have a few good years remaining has hit me with a real force . . . " (p. 129). How do her memories of her younger years inform her feelings of loss and how do they shape her approach to the years to come?

7. Several essays are entitled "I Just Want to Say" and go on to explore a specific topic. What do these pieces have in common?

8. Reread the lists ("What I Won't Miss" and "What I Will Miss") at the end of I Remember Nothing and create your own versions highlighting what you cherish—as well as you'd gladly give up.

9. If you have read I Feel Bad about My Neck, what changes do you see in Ephron's outlook and perceptions over the course of time between the two books?

I Think I Love You

By Allison Pearson

Wales, 1974. Petra and Sharon, two thirteen-year-old girls, are obsessed with David Cassidy. His fan magazine is their Bible, and some days his letters are the only things that keep them going as they struggle through the humiliating daily rituals of adolescence—confronting their bewildering new bodies, fighting with mothers who don't understand them at all. Together they tackle the Ultimate David Cassidy Quiz, a contest whose winners will be flown to America to meet Cassidy in person.

London, 1998. Petra is pushing forty, on the brink of divorce, and fighting with her own thirteen-year-old daughter when she discovers a dusty letter in her mother's closet declaring her the winner of the contest she and Sharon had labored over with such hope and determination. More than twenty years later, twenty pounds heavier, bruised by grief and the disappointments of middle age, Petra reunites with Sharon for an all-expenses-paid trip to Las Vegas to meet their teen idol at last, and finds her life utterly transformed.

"A delightful, giddy novel. . . . [Pearson] finds those universal chords, the stuff of great novels." —Los Angeles Times

ABOUT THE AUTHOR: **Allison Pearson**, an award-winning journalist and author, is a staff writer for the *London Daily Telegraph*. Her first novel, *I Don't Know How She Does It*, became an international bestseller and was translated into thirty-two languages. It is now a major motion picture, adapted by Aline Brosh McKenna and starring Sarah Jessica Parker, Greg Kinnear, Pierce Brosnan, Olivia Munn, and Christina Hendricks. Her most recent novel, *I Think I Love You*, is set to become a stage musical. Allison has given inspirational speeches around the world on women's issues and she can be contacted via her website www.allisonpearson.co.uk. She is a patron of Camfed, a charity that supports the education of more than a million African girls (www.camfed.org). Pearson lives in Cambridge with her husband and their two children.

September 2011 | Trade Paperback | Fiction | 416 pp | $14.95 | ISBN 9781400076918
Anchor | readinggroupcenter.com
Also available as: eBook and Audiobook

CONVERSATION STARTERS

1. What do you think this novel is about—love, illusion, friendship?

2. Zelda says to Bill, "Fantasy is an important part of growing up." How does this prove true for Petra? And for Bill?

3. Why does the author include articles from *The Essential David Cassidy Magazine*? What point is Pearson making?

4. "Honestly, it's amazing the things you can know about someone you don't know." Bill knows facts about David Cassidy because it's his job. Why do the girls study David so closely?

5. The girls lie to each other out of adolescent fear. Why does Bill lie to Ruth?

6. What does Petra learn about her friends at White City? What does she learn from her mother's response?

7. Discuss the pair of epigraphs on the opening page of Part Two. What impression do you get from their juxtaposition?

8. Petra thinks about *hiraeth*, the yearning for home. How does this relate to what ultimately happens with Sharon? With Bill?

9. What has Petra learned about motherhood from her own mother? In what ways is she like Greta?

10. How does Sharon help Petra get over Marcus?

11. "Never underestimate the wish not to know," Bill says to Petra. What does he mean? How does this apply to both Bill and Petra?

12. What is the significance of Petra's work with Ashley, the Girl That Nobody Loves? How does music heal Petra?

13. What did Bill get out of "being" David Cassidy? How did it benefit him, and how did it harm him?

14. Sharon likens her faith in *The Essential David Cassidy Magazine* to belief in the Bible. What does she mean? Were the girls choosing to believe?

15. Why does Petra take Bill's revelation about his work as a betrayal? Why doesn't Sharon?

16. Petra realizes her feelings about Greta have changed. What brings about this shift?

17. How does Pearson's afterword affect your feelings toward the novel as a whole?

Jerusalem Maiden
By Talia Carner

Esther Kaminsky knows that her duty is to marry young and produce many sons to help hasten the Messiah's arrival: that is what expected of young ultra-Orthodox women in Jerusalem at the end of the Ottoman Empire's rule. But when a teacher catches Esther's extraordinary doodling and gives her art lessons, Esther wonders if God has a special destiny for her: maybe she is meant to be an artist, not a mother; maybe she is meant to travel to Paris, not stay in Jerusalem. However, Esther sacrifices her own yearnings and devotes herself instead to following God's path as an obedient "Jerusalem maiden."

In the coming years, Esther struggles between comfort and repression in God's decrees, trusting the rituals of faith while suppressing her desires—until a surprising opportunity forces itself into her pre-ordained path. As her beliefs clash with the passions she has staved off her entire life, Esther must confront the hard questions: What is faith? Is there such thing as destiny? And to whom must she be true, to God or to herself?

"Talia Carner is a skillful and heartfelt storyteller who takes the reader on journey of the senses, into a world long forgotten." —**Jennifer Lauck, author of *Blackbird***

"Talia Carner's story captivates at every level, heart and mind." —**Jacquelyn Mitchard, author of *The Deep End of the Ocean***

ABOUT THE AUTHOR: **Talia Carner** is formerly the publisher of *Savvy Woman* magazine and a lecturer at international women economic forums. Carner's addictions include chocolate, ballet, hats—and social justice.

June 2011 | Trade Paperback | Fiction | 464 pp | $14.99 | ISBN 9780062004376
Harper Paperbacks | harpercollins.com | taliacarner.com
Also available as: eBook

CONVERSATION STARTERS

1. "The Greenwald girl" represents a concept of a young woman who followed her heart—and her non-Jewish lover—and brought a chain of disasters upon her family. Discuss Esther's action in light of this concept. Did she become "A Greenwald girl?"

2. Girls' innocence and purity are sacred in the ultra-Orthodox world of *Jerusalem Maiden*. Even today, many women in religious societies—Jewish, Christian, Hindu or Islam—live in even worse oppressive enclaves both in the West and in the Middle East, Asia and Africa. What are the tools used to control them in various places? Do these women share responsibility for their own insulation?

3. Esther does not desert her faith. She only rebels against the religious establishment. Have you experienced that gap?

4. Discuss the relationship between Esther and her mother during Esther's adolescence—and her view of that relationship as an adult. What were her mother's expectations, and what were Esther's?

5. When Aba recites *Woman of Valor* from the Book of Proverbs, Esther finds the expectations unattainable. What expectations exist today that reflect an unfeasibility similar to that of the *Woman of Valor*?

6. Twice in the novel Esther physically emerges from a dark place where she connected with her ancestors—at Rachel's Tomb and at Hezekiah Tunnel. Discuss the physical and spiritual illumination. Have you had similar experiences?

7. Esther's marriage to Nathan was not a bad one. She was comfortable and safe. Yet she was willing to throw it all away. Discuss her character and her dissatisfaction with what would have been many women's dream.

8. Esther's relationship with guilt fluctuates as she ages, accompanying rebellion, acquiescence, indignation and impetuousness. Throughout her life, how do her desires produce guilt, and how does she reconcile it at each step?

9. Esther's sojourn in Paris is supposed to be a vacation. Discuss the point at which it turns to abandonment of her children. Also, is her settling in Paris a betrayal of the Holy Land?

10. Even in today's open, free society, many women do not follow their hearts or their dreams to discover "The Primordial Light." Discuss what it takes for a woman to focus and to fully develop her talents.

11. In the end, Esther gives up the only two things she loves and which let her be who she is. Discuss her double sacrifice. What kind of a woman will she be in Jaffa and what life will she have back there?

The Legacy

By Katherine Webb

When they were children, Erica Calcott and her sister, Beth, spent their summer holidays at Storton Manor. Now, following the death of their grandmother, they have returned to the grand, imposing house in Wiltshire, England. Unable to stem the tide of childhood memories that arise as she sorts through her grandmother's belongings, Erica thinks back to the summer her cousin Henry vanished mysteriously from the estate, an event that tore their family to pieces. It is time, she believes, to lay the past to rest, bring her sister some peace, and finally solve the mystery of her cousin's disappearance.

But sifting through remnants of a bygone time is bringing a secret family history to light—one that stretches back over a century, to a beautiful society heiress in Oklahoma, a haunting, savage land across the ocean. And as past and present converge, Erica and Beth must come to terms with two shocking acts of betrayal . . . and the heartbreaking legacy they left behind.

"Stunning, unforgettable. . . . Webb's skillful, urgent writing is impossible to put down and more impossible to forget." — ***Booklist* (starred review)**

ABOUT THE AUTHOR: **Katherine Webb** was born in 1977 and grew up in rural Hampshire, England. She studied history at Durham University, has spent time living in London and Venice, and now lives in Berkshire, England. Having worked as a waitress, au pair, personal assistant, potter, bookbinder, library assistant, and formal housekeeper at a manor house, she now writes full-time.

September 2011 | Trade Paperback | Fiction | 496 pp | $14.99 | ISBN 9780062007730
Harper Paperbacks | harpercollins.com
Also available as: eBook

CONVERSATION STARTERS

1. How has the disappearance of their cousin Henry affected Erica and Beth Calcott? How about the other members of their family?

2. What is the relationship between Erica and Beth as adults, as compared to when they were children? Have their roles changed?

3. How did Erica feel about Dinny when they were younger? Why do you think Erica is still attracted to him now?

4. Do you find Caroline Massey to be a sympathetic character? Do you feel that she and Corin Massey were a good match? Why or why not?

5. Why is Caroline jealous of Magpie? Is there any justification for what she ends up doing to Magpie and her family?

6. Meredith, Erica and Beth's grandmother, is described as not a particularly warm or maternal woman. Why do you think she is that way? How much of it can be attributed to how her own mother, Caroline, brought her up?

7. Were you surprised to learn of Harry's true identity? Why or why not? What were the clues that led you to this revelation?

8. Do you agree with Erica and Beth's decision to keep the truth about Harry to themselves? In your opinion, is Harry better off this way?

9. Although present-day England and early 20th-century Oklahoma Territory seem very different, what similarities can you find between these two settings? For example, how about the way in which Dinny's family and Joe Ponca's family are treated?

10. What is the legacy that Caroline Massey has passed down to her descendants?

The Lonely Polygamist
By Brady Udall

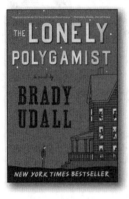

Golden Richards, husband to four wives, father to twenty-eight children, is having the mother of all midlife crises. His construction business is failing, and his family has grown into an overpopulated mini-dukedom beset with insurrection and rivalry. Brady Udall, one of our finest American fiction writers, tells the poignant yet wonderfully comic story of a deeply faithful man who becomes entangled in an affair that threatens his family's future. Beautifully written, keenly observed, and populated with characters that engage us to the fullest, *The Lonely Polygamist* is an unforgettable story of an American family—with its inevitable dysfunctionality, heartbreak, and comedy—pushed to its outer limits.

"[An] exceptional tale of an exceptional family." —**The New York Times Book Review**

"A superb performance . . . Udall's polished storytelling and sterling cast of perfectly realized and flawed characters make this a serious contender for Great American Novel status." —**Publishers Weekly** (**starred review**)

"Udall masterfully portrays the hapless foibles and tragic yearnings of our fellow humans." —**San Francisco Chronicle**

ABOUT THE AUTHOR: **Brady Udall** is the author of *Letting Loose the Hounds* and *The Miracle Life of Edgar Mint*, an international bestseller. His work has appeared in *The Paris Review*, *Playboy*, *GQ* and *Esquire*, and his stories and essays have been featured on National Public Radio's *This American Life*. He teaches in the MFA program at Boise State University, and lives in Boise, Idaho, and Teasdale, Utah, with his wife and children.

Sign up for W. W. Norton's Reading Group Newsletter,
e-mail readinggroup@wwnorton.com.

May 2011 | Trade Paperback | Fiction | 624 pp | $15.95 | ISBN 9780393339710
W.W. Norton & Company | wwnorton.com | bradyudall.com
Also available as: Hardcover and eBook

CONVERSATION STARTERS

1. What were your views on polygamy before reading the book? Did they change after you finished reading?

2. Discuss Golden's progression from lonely polygamist to social polygamist. How does a renewal of faith assist this transformation?

3. Compare and contrast Golden's behavior at the two funerals. How are they similar? In what ways are they different?

4. How does Glory affect the other family members and Golden in particular?

5. Discuss the motifs of creation and destruction that appear throughout the novel.

6. Do you think Rusty is a representative figure for all of the Richards children in the novel, or is he in some ways unique?

7. Trish is one of the most conflicted mothers in the novel. What do you think of her decision at the end? Was it the right thing to do?

8. How has the family changed at the conclusion of the novel? Do you think they are happy with their decisions?

9. Discuss Rose-of-Sharon's reaction to Rusty's accident. Do you think you would have reacted the same way if you were in her place?

10. Why do you think Golden isn't able to consummate his affair with Huila?

11. Physical appearance is described with exacting clarity throughout the novel. Golden is described as bucktoothed and "Sasquatch," and Glory as "lopsided" and "overstuffed." Why do you think there is such a heightened awareness of the body?

12. What is the effect of polygamy on the women in the novel? How do you think their lives and personalities would be different if they weren't in a polygamous relationship?

Lowcountry Summer

By Dorothea Benton Frank

Return to Tall Pines in the long-awaited sequel to Dorothea Benton Frank's beloved bestseller *Plantation*. *Lowcountry Summer* is the story of the changing anatomy of a family after the loss of its matriarch, sparkling with the inimitable Dot Frank's warmth and humor—as a new generation stumbles, survives, and reveals their secrets by the banks of the mighty Edisto River.

On the occasion of her 46th birthday, Caroline Wimbley Levine is concerned about filling the large shoes of her late, force-of-nature mother, Miss Lavinia, the former Queen of Tall Pines Plantation. Still, Caroline loves a challenge—and she simply will not be fazed by the myriad family catastrophes surrounding her. She'll deal with brother Trip's tricky romantic entanglements, son Eric and his mysterious girlfriend, and go toe-to-toe with alcoholic Frances Mae and her four hellcats without batting an eye, becoming more like Miss Lavinia every day . . . which is not an entirely good thing.

"*Lowcountry Summer has it all: a sassy, lovable narrator; great, believable characters; laugh-out-loud lines; page-turning action; and surprising plot twists. In other words, it's Dorothea Benton Frank at her best!*"
—**Cassandra King**

ABOUT THE AUTHOR: **Dorothea Benton Frank** is the *New York Times* best-selling author of *Lowcountry Summer, Return to Sullivans Island, Bulls Island, The Land of Mango Sunsets, The Christmas Pearl, Full of Grace, Pawleys Island, Shem Creek, Isle of Palms, Plantation* and *Sullivans Island*. The author, who was born and raised on Sullivans Island in South Carolina and has been married forever to Peter Frank, currently divides her time between New Jersey and the Lowcountry of South Carolina. You can find Dorothea on Facebook.

April 2011 | Trade Paperback | Fiction | 384 pp | $13.99 | ISBN 9780062020734
William Morrow Paperbacks | harpercollins.com | dotfrank.com
Also available as: eBook and Audiobook

CONVERSATION STARTERS

1. Describe Caroline's relationship with her brother and the rest of her clan. How do the young people in the novel behave towards each other and towards their elders?

2. What things might Lavinia—coming from a different generation—have taken for granted that Caroline cannot? What accounts for these differences? How do the three generations of Wimbley women compare and contrast with one another?

3. Caroline firmly believes in good manners and propriety. Why? Do you think these attributes are out of date—or are they more necessary than ever in today's world?

4. Tradition is also important to Caroline. "Families like ours and Miss Sweetie's never downsized and moved to condos in Boca. Sell the blood-soaked land our ancestors had died to protect? Never in a million years!" How does such loyalty shape a person's life? When can loyalty to a cause, a place, a person become destructive?

5. Dorothea Benton Frank uses the Lowcounty as both a setting and a character in the novel. How does this place shape its inhabitants? How would you describe it? Have you ever had a connection with a place like Caroline does with Tall Pines Plantation? Would having such a link be comforting or confining?

6. Compare Caroline with her sister in law, Frances Mae. Why do they dislike each other? How can the two join together in the name of the family? Could such a bond be strengthened? Can it last?

7. The bond—or lack of one—between parents and children—is a prevalent theme of *Lowcountry Summer*. What is Trip's relationship with his daughters? Why is he so helpless to contain them? What did the girls think about their mother? What makes a good mother?

8. Did Caroline overreact when she discovered her other niece, Linnie, was smoking pot at Belle's graduation party? Could she have handled the situation better? Did Linnie deserve the slap she got from her aunt? Millie doesn't like hitting and slapping, "But maybe sometimes a chile needs something to shake 'em up. Specially that knucklehead [Linnie]." What do you think of this?

9. What about Caroline's feelings for Matthew—why was she so reluctant to admit how she really felt about him? What do you think the future holds for them?

10. The book is filled with several rites of passage: weddings, funerals, a graduation. How is Caroline's position as matriarch defined by these rites?

The Maid

A Novel of Joan of Arc

By Kimberly Cutter

The girl who led an army, the peasant who crowned a king, the maid who became a legend.

It is the fifteenth century, and the tumultuous Hundred Years' War rages on. France is under siege, English soldiers tear through the countryside destroying all who cross their path, and Charles VII, the uncrowned king, has neither the strength nor the will to rally his army. And in the quiet of her parents' garden in Domrémy, a peasant girl sees a spangle of light and hears a powerful voice speak her name. Jehanne.

The story of Jehanne d'Arc, the visionary and saint who believed she had been chosen by God, who led an army and saved her country, has captivated our imagination for centuries. But the story of Jehanne—the girl—whose sister was murdered by the English, who sought an escape from a violent father and a forced marriage, who taught herself to ride and fight, and who somehow found the courage and tenacity to persuade first one, then two, then thousands to follow her, is at once thrilling, unexpected, and heartbreaking.

Rich with unspoken love and battlefield valor, *The Maid* is a novel about the power and uncertainty of faith, and the exhilarating and devastating consequences of fame.

"Pacy enough to outstrip any cliché about Saint Joan, yet also tender portrait of a young girl drawn into a hateful destiny." —**Michelle Lovric, author of *The Book of Human Skin***

ABOUT THE AUTHOR: **Kimberly Cutter** received her MFA from the University of Virginia. She was the West Coast editor for *W Magazine* for four years. She has written for *Harper's Bazaar, W, Vanity Fair, New York Magazine,* and *Marie Claire,* where she is currently a contributing editor. She lives in Brooklyn, New York.

October 2011 | Hardcover | Fiction | 304 pp | $26.00 | ISBN 9780547427522
Houghton Mifflin Harcourt | hmhbooks.com | themaidbook.com
Available as: eBook

1. How does Jehanne's faith evolve? How do others view her faith? How did you?

2. Could Jehanne have performed such feats today as she did then? Are there contemporary equivalents? If someone came to you today and told you she was hearing voices, what would you do? Would you believe her, or commit her? Would it make a difference if that person were a person of faith, either Catholic or Muslim or Jewish?

3. Look at the instances in which Jehanne performs violent acts. How are these portrayed? Do you believe Jehanne killed in battle, as *The Maid* suggests? "'You miraculous creature, you've done it.' 'God did it,' Jehanne said, thinking of the dead man with the knife in his throat. Thinking, *But who did that? Did He or did I?*" (p. 209). Is it possible to kill and still be pure, a saint? What absolves Jehanne of those murders, if so?

4. Why are the men's clothing and the suit of armor so important to Jehanne? How does she transform according to what she has on? How does clothing define us?

5. "You think there's such a thing as a good war, a justified war? You think there's such a thing as honest blood?" (p. 266). Does Jehanne believe there is? Do you? Compare the war Jehanne fought to the wars ongoing today. Are there any similarities?

6. Why do the voices desert Jehanne? What sort of doubt does Jehanne struggle with and why do you think she had to go through that? Did Jehanne ever err in her faith or her responsibilities? Were these human fallibilities? What elevated her to sainthood?

7. Jehanne was burned at the stake, the townspeople shouting, "Witch!" What is the fine line between being a witch and a saint? How does that tie into Jehanne's doubt later in the novel? Consider also the many other stories of witch trials and how they were similar to or different than Jehanne's trial.

8. Why is it so important that Jehanne remain a virgin? Was she? Does it matter?

9. Did Jehanne really hear voices or was she mentally ill? What do you think? What does the author believe?

10. How is the Joan of Arc portrayed in *The Maid* different or similar to the Joan of Arc you knew before reading the novel? What did you learn? What makes Kimberly Cutter's version of events unique? Can you learn more from a novel than you can from a biography? What liberties does the novelist have in situations like this?

Mama Ruby
By Mary Monroe

Growing up in Shreveport, Louisiana, Ruby Jean Upshaw is the kind of girl who knows what she wants and knows how to get it. By the time she's fifteen, Ruby has developed a taste for fast men and cheap liquor, and not even her preacher daddy can set her straight. Most everyone in the neighborhood knows you don't cross Ruby. Only Othella Mae Cartier, daughter of the town tramp, understands what makes Ruby tick.

When Ruby discovers she's in the family way, she's scared for the first time in her life. After hiding her growing belly with baggy dresses, Ruby secretly gives birth to a baby girl at Othella's house. With few choices, Othella talks Ruby into giving the child away and to run off with her to New Orleans. But nothing can erase Ruby's memories of the child she lost—or quell her simmering rage at Othella for persuading her to let her precious baby go.

If there's a fine line between best friend and worst nightmare, Ruby is surely treading it. Because someday, there will be a reckoning. And when it comes, Othella will learn the hard way that no one knows how to exact revenge quite like Ruby Jean Upshaw.

"Monroe's characters deal with their situations with a weary worldliness and fatalism that reveal their vulnerability as well as their flaws. Although this works as a stand-alone title, fans of Monroe's The Upper Room *will be thrilled to see this prequel, which explains what made Mama Ruby the one-of-a-kind woman she is." —Booklist*

ABOUT THE AUTHOR: **Mary Monroe** is the third child of Alabama sharecroppers, and the first and only member of her family to finish high school. Mary never attended college or any writing classes. Her first novel, *The Upper Room*, was published in 1985 and was widely reviewed throughout the U.S. and in Great Britain. Monroe loves to travel. She has lived in Oakland since 1984.

June 2011 | Hardcover | Fiction | 416 pp | $24.00 | ISBN 9780758238610
Dafina | kensingtonbooks.com | marymonroe.org
Also available as: eBook and Audiobook

CONVERSATION STARTERS

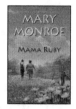

1. Do you think that if Ruby's overly religious parents hadn't been so strict, she would not have been so promiscuous and eager to be part of Othella's wild crowd?

2. Do you think that Ruby should have defied Simone and Othella and kept the baby? Do you think that it was wrong for Simone to turn the baby over to that asylum orphanage to keep her from being "shunned" by Ruby's family and friends for being a "rapist's" child?

3. There were several hints along the way that Ruby's Bible thumping father, Reverend Upshaw, was a philanderer. Were you surprised when Ruby and Othella caught him in bed with Othella's mother?

4. Ruby used the knowledge of her father's affair as leverage against him, so he eagerly allowed her to quit school and move from Shreveport to New Orleans with Othella. Do you think that Reverend Upshaw should have confessed his indiscretion to his wife, and not let Ruby blackmail him into letting her leave home?

5. After Ruby and Othella escaped from Glenn Boates, things went from bad to worse for them. Their only choices were to go back home, live on the streets of New Orleans, or work in Miss Maureen's brothel. Do you think that they should have returned to their parents' homes?

6. During the time period that this story is set in, it was unacceptable for a black person to "sass" a white person, let alone assault one. Were you glad that Ruby didn't let that stop her from standing up for herself when she had to deal with hostile whites? Do you think she went too far when she beat up the man who had attacked her and Miss Maureen?

7. Othella's husband, Eugene, did not treat her well. But Ruby's husband, Roy, treated her like a queen, until she caught him with another woman. Did Ruby overreact by shooting him with the same gun that he made her carry for protection?

8. On the day that Othella went into labor at Ruby's house, Ruby gave Othella a letter from her mother that had been put in Ruby's mailbox by mistake. This letter contained some crucial information that would have made a huge difference in Ruby's and Othella's lives. Unfortunately, Othella delayed reading that letter, and she would regret it for the rest of her life. Did the information in the letter surprise you?

9. Because of Ruby's violent history, volatile personality, and peculiar habits, do you think that Ruby's daughter was better off not having Ruby in her life?

Minding Frankie

By Maeve Binchy

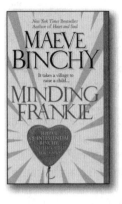

Maeve Binchy is back with a tale of joy, heartbreak and hope, about a motherless girl collectively raised by a close-knit Dublin community.

When Noel learns that his terminally ill former flame is pregnant with his child, he agrees to take guardianship of the baby girl once she's born. But as a single father battling demons of his own, Noel can't do it alone. Fortunately, he has a competent, caring network of friends, family and neighbors: Lisa, his unlucky-in-love classmate, who moves in with him to help him care for little Frankie around the clock; his American cousin, Emily, always there with a pep talk; the newly retired Dr. Hat, with more time on his hands than he knows what to do with; Dr. Declan and Fiona and their baby son, Frankie's first friend; and many eager babysitters, including old friends Signora and Aidan and Frankie's doting grandparents, Josie and Charles. But not everyone is pleased with the unconventional arrangement, especially a nosy social worker, Moira, who is convinced that Frankie would be better off in a foster home. Now it's up to Noel to persuade her that everyone in town has something special to offer when it comes to minding Frankie.

"One of Binchy's best works. She harmoniously handles a diverse group of characters, the good deeds that characterize life in Ireland are believable, and the ending is sweet." —**Susan Rogers,** *Newark Star-Ledger*

"Binchy's world view is a large, benevolent one, and the reader is happier for it." —**Laurie Hertzel,** *Minneapolis Star-Tribune*

ABOUT THE AUTHOR: **Maeve Binchy** is the author of *Nights of Rain and Stars, Scarlet Feather, Quentins, Light a Penny Candle, Circle of Friends,* and *Tara Road* (An Oprah Book Club Selection) and many other bestselling books. Maeve has now retired as a journalist and columnist for the *Irish Times* and lives in Dalkey, Ireland, and London with her husband, writer Gordon Snell.

December 2011 | Mass Market Paperback | Fiction | 480 pp | $7.99 | ISBN 9780307475497
Anchor | readinggroupcenter.com | maevebinchy.com
Also available as: eBook and Audiobook

CONVERSATION STARTERS

1. Have you read any of Maeve Binchy's other novels? How does this one compare?
2. If you've read other Binchy books, which characters did you recognize? Are there any you'd like to see in a future novel?
3. There are many parents in the book. Who would you say does the best job, and why?
4. There are a number of recent retirees, voluntary and otherwise, who become an important part of Frankie's life. What kind of roles do her grandparents, Josie and Charles, take on? What about Dr. Hat and Muttie? More generally, what do the very young and the very mature have to offer each other? Which generation do you think needs the other more?
5. "Emily told herself that she must not try to change the world. . . . But there were some irresistible forces that could never be fought with logic and practicality. Emily Lynch knew this for certain." What "irresistible forces" does she mean? How does she fight them?
6. It's clear what Noel gets from his relationship with Emily, but what does she get? How does the effect of alcoholism bond them?
7. Discuss Lisa's relationship with Anton. Why is she so oblivious to his less attractive qualities? What is her turning point?
8. Why is Moira so obsessed with Frankie's fate? Is it just fear, or is there something more going on?
9. How does Moira define "family"? How does Emily?
10. Lisa says to Moira, "I have a lot of worries and considerations in my life, but minding Frankie sort of grounds me. It gives it all some purpose, if you know what I mean." Among Frankie's caretakers, who else might say this?
11. Discuss the ethics of Moira's dealings with Eddie Kennedy. Should she have told him about her father?
12. Anton says to Lisa, "I'm not the villain here, you know," and she responds, "I know. That's why I'm angry. I got it so wrong . . . ." What does she mean?
13. What did you think of Di Kelly's reason for staying with her husband? What would you have done?
14. What is your opinion of Noel's decision to get a DNA test? How would you have handled the results he received?
15. Many of the characters go through major upheavals in their lives. Who responds best, and why? Whose attitude changes the most?

Miss Timmins' School for Girls

By Nayana Currimbhoy

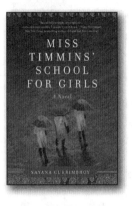

A murder at a British boarding school in the hills of western India launches a young teacher on the journey of a lifetime.

In 1974, three weeks before her twenty-first birthday, Charulata Apte arrives at Miss Timmins' School for Girls in Panchgani. Shy, sheltered, and running from a scandal that disgraced her Brahmin family, Charu finds herself teaching Shakespeare to rich Indian girls in a boarding school still run like an outpost of the British Empire. In this small, foreign universe, Charu is drawn to the charismatic teacher Moira Prince, who introduces her to pot-smoking hippies, rock 'n' roll, and freedoms she never knew existed.

Then one monsoon night, a body is found at the bottom of a cliff, and the ordered worlds of school and town are thrown into chaos. When Charu is implicated in the murder—a case three intrepid schoolgirls take it upon themselves to solve—Charu's real education begins. A love story and a murder mystery, *Miss Timmins' School for Girls* is, ultimately, a coming-of-age tale set against the turbulence of the 1970s as it played out in one small corner of India.

"An irresistible novel that hurls forward at breathtaking speed toward an unpredictable climax." —**Thrity Umrigar, bestselling author of *The Space Between Us***

ABOUT THE AUTHOR: **Nayana Currimbhoy** was raised in India where she attended an all-girls boarding school in a fairly remote hill station. She moved to the U.S. in the early eighties, and has been a businesswoman and a freelance writer. She has written books, film scripts, and articles about many things, including architecture and design, and a biography of India Gandhi. *Miss Timmins' School for Girls* is her first novel. Nayana lives in New York City with her husband, an architect, and their teenage daughter.

July 2011 | Trade Paperback | Fiction | 512 pp | $14.99 | ISBN 9780061997747
Harper Paperbacks | harpercollins.com
Also available as: eBook

CONVERSATION STARTERS

1. In *Miss Timmins' School for Girls*, young Charu is suddenly exposed to Christian British-run boarding school, as well as to the iconoclastic hippie culture of the 1970s. "I watched my worlds collide," says Charu, "not in fire and brimstone as I had feared, but in comic relief." Do you think this is true of the book? What are the main cultural conflicts our heroine faces? Are they all resolved through humor?

2. Charu's parents have tried to protect their beloved only child from a world they consider cruel. Do you think they did her a disservice by limiting her exposure to the world at large? In what way do you think her cloistered upbringing led Charu to be seduced by Moira Prince?

3. In spite of her erratic behavior and dark past, do you think Moira Prince is presented as a sympathetic character? How does the author do this?

4. Charu, has a disfiguring mark on her face. This has made her into an intense, sensitive and secretive person, a watcher. How do you think this influences her actions, and ultimately, the resolution of the murder mystery?

5. When Charu mourns Prince, she finds herself humming "Ruby Tuesday" by the Rolling Stones. Do you find this incongruous? The soundtrack of the book is rock 'n' roll: The Beatles, the Rolling Stones, Cat Stevens, Bob Dylan and Jethro Tull. In your opinion, does this make the foreign landscape and culture more familiar to you? Does it resonate with a coming of age in America in the seventies?

6. One part of the book is narrated by Nandita, a 15-year-old school girl. How does the author use Nandita's voice to move the story further? Does Nandita's vision change your opinion of Charu? If so, how?

7. The principal of Miss Timmins', Miss Shirley Nelson, puts her reputation in the school above the life of her own daughter. What is it about the relationship between them that makes this believable?

8. The novel begins and ends on the same day, twelve years after the actual events take place. In the end of the prologue, Merch is planning to do something that night. What do you think he plans to do?

9. At the very end of the book, when Charu says, "It's all over now," what does she mean? In your opinion, what is Merch thinking of, when he asks "What is all over?" Do you think she is still thinking of the murder 12 years ago?

The Moment

By Douglas Kennedy

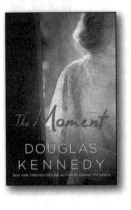

Thomas Nesbitt is a divorced writer in the midst of a rueful middle age. Living a very private life in Maine, in touch only with his daughter and still trying to recover from the end of a long marriage, his solitude is disrupted one wintry morning by the arrival of a box that is postmarked Berlin. The name on the box—Dussmann—unsettles him completely, for it belongs to the woman with whom he had an intense love affair twenty-six years ago in Berlin at a time when the city was cleaved in two and personal and political allegiances were frequently haunted by the deep shadows of the Cold War. Refusing initially to confront what he might find in that box, Thomas nevertheless is forced to grapple with a past he has never discussed with any living person and in the process relive those months in Berlin when he discovered, for the first and only time in his life, the full, extraordinary force of true love. But Petra Dussmann, the woman to whom he lost his heart, was not just a refugee from a police state, but also someone who lived with an ongoing sorrow that gradually rewrote both their destinies.

A love story of great epic sweep and immense emotional power, *The Moment* explores why and how we fall in love—and the way we project on to others that which our hearts so desperately seek.

*"Readers are bound to fall under the sway of this richly romantic novel set against the melancholy backdrop of a divided city." —**Booklist***

*"An observant, compassionate, and romantic portrait of emotional turmoil in troubled times." —**Publishers Weekly***

ABOUT THE AUTHOR: **Douglas Kennedy** is the author of ten novels, including the international bestseller *Leaving the World* and *The Moment*. His work has been translated into 22 languages, and in 2007 he received the French decoration of Chevalier de l'Ordre des Arts et des Lettres. He has two children and now divides his time between London, Paris, Berlin and Maine.

May 2011 | Hardcover | Fiction | 544 pp | $26.99 | ISBN 9781439180792
Atria | imprints.simonandschuster.biz/atria
pages.simonandschuster.com/douglas-kennedy
Also available as: eBook

CONVERSATION STARTERS

1. Thomas Nesbitt tells his daughter "the moment . . . it's a very over-rated place." Do you agree with this statement? How does Thomas's notion of the moment change over the course of the book?

2. Upon his arrival in Berlin, Thomas attends a concert and states, "You only begin to grasp the importance of an event—and its larger implications vis-à-vis your life—long after it has entered into that realm marked 'memory.'" Discuss this quotation in terms of Thomas's reflections on his time with Petra. Did Thomas realize what he had only after Petra was gone?

3. How does the time and setting of Thomas and Petra's love story add to the intensity of their relationship? Do you think the story would have been as powerful if it did not take place at the foot of the Berlin Wall?

4. Betrayal is a key element in *The Moment*. How are the main characters betrayed by each other? By those around them? When does Thomas realize whom he can actually trust?

5. What is superbia? Where and when does it occur in the book and to whom?

6. What were your initial reactions to how quickly Thomas and Petra's relationship was progressed? Do you think it was doomed to fail from the start? If Bubriski had never gotten involved, would they still be together?

7. What does snow symbolize in *The Moment*? Discuss the various scenes where snow is present including at the scene of Thomas's accident, his crossing back into West Berlin and his final ride back to his cabin.

8. Were you surprised that Thomas had to continually convince himself that his love with Petra was real? Do you agree with his notion "if you write, *everything* is material. And part of me felt that, by getting it all down . . . that, yes I had met the love of my life"?

9. Walter Bubriski informs Thomas that Petra is an agent of the Stasi. How does Bubriski's news shred the psychological wall Thomas had built regarding his love for Petra? Do you think Bubriski knew Petra's true back story?

10. Explain what Thomas means when he calls his love for Jan "qualified." Why did Jan opt to stay with Thomas even though she knew he loved someone else?

11. *The Moment* is three stories told from three different perspectives: Thomas's in the present day, Thomas's in the past, and Petra's. Why do you think the author chose to construct the novel in such a way?

My Name Is Memory

By Ann Brashares

Daniel has spent centuries falling in love with the same girl. Life after life, crossing continents and dynasties, he and Sophia (despite her changing name and form) have been drawn together—and he remembers it all. Daniel has "the memory," the ability to recall past lives and recognize souls of those he's previously known. It is a gift and a curse. For all the times that he and Sophia have been drawn together throughout history, they have also been torn painfully, fatally, apart.

But just when young Sophia (now "Lucy" in the present) finally begins to awaken to the secret of their shared past, the mysterious force that has always torn them apart reappears. Ultimately, they must come to understand what stands in the way of their love if they are ever to spend a lifetime together.

"A fantastical romance." —**Washington Post**

"We all like to believe in the consistency of love. And then along comes Ann Brashares to take the concept to a whole new level." —**Minneapolis Star Tribune**

ABOUT THE AUTHOR: **Ann Brashares** is the *New York Times* bestselling author of *The Sisterhood of the Traveling Pants, The Second Summer of the Sisterhood, Girls in Pants,* and *Forever in Blue,* and the adult novel *The Last Summer (of You and Me).* She lives in New York.

June 2011 | Trade Paperback | Fiction | 352 pp | $15.00 | ISBN 9781594485183
Riverhead Books | penguin.com | annbrashares.com
Also available as: eBook and Audiobook

1. *My Name Is Memory* unfolds in chapters alternating between Daniel and Lucy's voices. What did you think of this technique? Do you think the author captured both voices equally well? Was there one character whose point of view you preferred reading?

2. How do Lucy's experiences with her older sister Dana's mental illness affect her reaction to Daniel when he tells her about their past lives together? How much of her response do you think comes from fear? Do you think she wants to believe him?

3. Daniel insists on being called "Daniel" in each life, and he calls Lucy "Sophia," the name she had when he first fell in love with her. Why is he so attached to using these names? What is their significance to him? What changes at the novel's end that allows him to finally call her "Lucy"?

4. Daniel talks about human beings' ability to recognize other people's souls, and says, "Our souls reveal themselves in our face and body . . . Choose a person's face and study it carefully. . . . Ask yourself what you know about the person, and if you open yourself to the information, you will find you know an overwhelming amount" (p. 55). Do you think this is true?

5. When Lucy looks back on her first meeting with Daniel she is filled with regret. "It must have been painful for him to realize [Sophia] was gone, replaced by a coward" (p. 196). Do you agree with Lucy's assessment of herself that she's a coward, or would you consider her brave? Does her level of bravery change over the course of the book? How or why?

6. Brashares writes, as Daniel thinks he's about to lose Lucy, "If you didn't have a choice, you had to make a choice. If you didn't have options, you made some. You couldn't just let the world happen to you" (p. 505). Is this something he has always believed? Is it advice he has followed? To what consequences? How has it shaped his collection of lives?

7. At the beginning of the novel, Daniel says that despite all his lives, "I've never had a child, and I've never gotten old. I don't know why" (p. 2). Why do you think these two rites of passage, so integrally a part of the human condition, have been denied him? Do you think he will get to experience both of these things in his "ultimate" life? Is the life with Lucy the one he's been waiting for?

The Ninth Wife

By Amy Stolls

What sane woman would consider becoming any man's ninth wife?

Bess Gray is a thirty-five-year-old folklorist and amateur martial artist living in Washington, DC. Just as she's about to give up all hope of marriage, she meets Rory, a charming Irish musician, and they fall in love. But Rory is a man with a secret, which he confesses to Bess when he asks for her hand: He's been married eight times before. Shocked, Bess embarks on a quest she feels she must undertake before she can give him an answer.

With her bickering grandparents (married sixty-five years), her gay neighbor (himself a mystery), a shar-pei named Stella, and a mannequin named Peace, Bess sets out on a cross-country journey—unbeknownst to Rory—to seek out and question the wives who came before. What she discovers about her own past is far more than she bargained for.

The Ninth Wife is a smart, funny, eye-opening tale of love, marriage, and the power of stories to unlock the true meaning of home and family.

"The Ninth Wife *is a vibrant, nuanced novel about marriage, identity and the moment when we realize that the shimmer of fantasy pales next to the tumultuous reality of ordinary, everyday happiness.*" —**Carolyn Parkhurst, bestselling author of** *The Dogs of Babel*

ABOUT THE AUTHOR: **Amy Stolls**'s young adult novel *Palms to the Ground* was published in 2005 to critical acclaim and was a Parents' Choice Gold Award winner. A former environmental journalist who covered the Exxon Valdez oil spill in Alaska, she is currently a literature program officer for the National Endowment for the Arts. She lives in Washington, DC, with her husband and son.

May 2011 | Trade Paperback | Fiction | 496 pp | $14.99 | ISBN 9780061851896
Harper Paperbacks | harpercollins.com | amystolls.com
Also available as: eBook

CONVERSATION STARTERS

1. The novel opens with Bess's karate teacher saying, "Pick a partner ... and get a tombstone." Metaphorically, that's what society often urges us to do: find someone, get married, and stay married for life. But how difficult is that to do in this day and age?

2. Bess is a thirty-something living in a city with an ache for companionship and kids, and bad luck in the dating realm. She tells Rory she feels like a cliché. Do you think current portrayals of single women in the media help or hamper the happiness of real-life single women?

3. Do you think Rory should have told Bess about his ex-wives on their first date or soon after? Likewise, do you think Bess should have told him she was seeking out his ex-wives? If he had told her not to, should she have abandoned her plans?

4. To what degree should our past define us? Rory argues that you don't have to know much about someone's past to understand that person in the present. Bess argues, on the other hand, that we're a sum of our experiences and that we need to understand those experiences to understand ourselves and each other. Whom do you agree with?

5. Bess feels she knows too little about her own ancestry to feel connected to a past. How does your cultural heritage—or, as for Bess, a lack of cultural heritage—contribute to your self-identity?

6. Why do you think Millie is physically harming Irv? Why do you think Irv is keeping quiet about it?

7. Bess is sometimes frustrated with how many secrets Millie, Irv, Cricket, and Rory keep from her. Do you think it's wrong for loved ones to keep secrets from each other?

8. In an email to Bess, Dao asks: "What can we truly know?" What does she mean by that? What message is Dao ultimately trying to convey? What has Bess learned throughout her journey that might help her answer this question?

9. Would you, in the end, marry someone who has been married eight times before? Is your answer different now that you've read *The Ninth Wife*? What would be some of the determining factors in your decision? What if he/she were married three times?

10. Have Bess and Rory learned what it takes to make a marriage last into old age? Do you think their marriage has a good chance of succeeding?

The Oracle of Stamboul

By Michael David Lukas

Late in the summer of 1877, a flock of purple-and-white hoopoes suddenly appears over the town of Constanta on the Black Sea, and Eleonora Cohen is ushered into the world by a pair of midwives who arrive just before her birth. But joy is mixed with tragedy, for Eleonora's mother dies soon after the birth.

Raised by her doting father, Yakob, and her stern stepmother, Ruxandra, Eleonora spends her early years daydreaming and doing housework—until the moment she teaches herself to read.

When Yakob sets off by boat for Stamboul on business, eight-year-old Eleonora, stows away in one of his trunks. On the shores of the Bosporus a new life awaits. For in the narrow streets of Stamboul—a city at the crossroads of the world—intrigue and gossip are currency, and people are not always what they seem. Eleonora's tutor may be a spy. The kindly though elusive Moncef Bey has a past history of secret societies and political maneuvering. And what is to be made of the eccentric, charming Sultan Abdulhamid II himself, beleaguered by friend and foe alike as his multi-ethnic empire crumbles?

The Oracle of Stamboul is a marvelously evocative, magical historical novel that will transport readers to another time and place—romantic, exotic, yet remarkably similar to our own.

"Lukas . . . brings a raconteur's sense of storytelling, a traveler's eye for color and a scholar's sense of history to his first novel. . . . Lukas has given us a Turkish delight."—**San Francisco Chronicle**

ABOUT THE AUTHOR: **Michael David Lukas** has been a Fulbright scholar in Turkey, a late-shift proofreader in Tel Aviv, and a Rotary scholar in Tunisia. He is a graduate of Brown University and the University of Maryland. Lukas lives in Oakland, less than a mile from where he was born.

August 2011 | Trade Paperback | Fiction | 320 pp | $13.99 | ISBN 9780062012104
Harper Perennial | harpercollins.com | michaeldavislukas.com
Also available as: eBook and Audiobook

CONVERSATION STARTERS

1. A prophecy foretold the birth of a girl like Eleonora Cohen. Do you believe in mystical propositions such as prophecies? Do you think the events surrounding her birth were truly foretold or just coincidence? Why do we in the West dismiss the idea of prophets and prophecies? Have we lost something in doing so?

2. Eleonora's life touched those of many adults, including her father, Yakob. Talk about their bond.

3. Eleonora's favorite saga was a seven-volume epic called *The Hourglass*. What lessons did she learn from the novel? How did the book impact the events that followed?

4. "If there was one thing she learned from *The Hourglass* it was that you should always follow the dictates of your own heart." Do you agree with this? What happens when we don't follow the dictates of our hearts? When might we choose not to do so?

5. The sultan disagreed with his closest councilor on the methods of effective governance. For the sultan, "an effective ruler needed more than anything to maintain a proper distance from the events that occurred within his domain." Do you agree with this? Can a leader become too caught up in the details? But might ignoring details be detrimental for good leadership?

6. Why was the sultan willing to grant Eleanora an audience? What advice do you think she gave him? If you heard that the president met with someone like Eleonora, what would you think?

7. When Eleonora discovers something incriminating about the reverend, she isn't sure whether or not to confide in the Bey. "Plato would seem to think she should. Truth is the beginning of every good to the gods, and of every good to man. Then again, there was Tertullian. Truth engenders hatred of the truth. As soon as it appears it is the enemy." Discuss both of these viewpoints. Which do you side with more?

8. Another philosophical debate Eleonora has is between doing something wrong and not yet doing the right thing. "Was there a difference between these two sins?" she wonders. How would you answer this question?

9. After her tragedy, Eleonora stops speaking. What does being "voiceless" offer her? If you chose not to speak for a few days, what might you learn? Do you think it would make you a better listener?

10. Why did Eleonora make the choice she did at the story's end? Was she walking away from her "fate"—or was she ultimately saving her life?

The Oriental Wife

By Evelyn Toynton

The story of two assimilated Jewish children from Nuremberg who flee Hitler's Germany and struggle to put down roots elsewhere. When they meet up again in New York, they fall in love both with each other and with America, believing they have found a permanent refuge. But just when it looks as though nothing can ever touch them again, their lives are shattered by a freakish accident and a betrayal that will reverberate into the life of their American daughter. In its portrait of the immigrant experience, and of the tragic gulf between generations, *The Oriental Wife* illuminates the collision of American ideals of freedom and happiness with certain sterner old world virtues.

"*A first-rate literary work and a character study of loss.*"—**Kirkus Reviews**

"*The Oriental Wife is a clear-eyed but tender, always intelligent, and beautifully observed group portrait of German Jews, their lives shattered by the Third Reich, painfully finding their way in England and the New World. A remarkable and virtuous achievement!*" —**Louis Begley, author of, most recently, Why the Dreyfus Affair Matters**

"*An intense and moving story of post–Holocaust Jewish immigrants.*" —**Booklist**

ABOUT THE AUTHOR: **Evelyn Toynton**'s last novel, *Modern Art,* was a *New York Times* Notable Book of the Year and was long-listed for the Ambassador Award of the English-Speaking Union. Her work has appeared in *Harper's, The Atlantic, The American Scholar,* the *Times Literary Supplement,* and the *New York Times Book Review,* as well as a number of anthologies, including *Rereadings* and *Mentors, Muses & Monsters.* Her book on Jackson Pollock will be published in 2012 by Yale University Press as part of its Icons of America series. She lives in Norfolk, England.

July 2011 | Trade Paperback | Fiction | 288 pp | $15.95 | ISBN 9781590514412
Other Press | otherpress.com
Also available as: eBook

CONVERSATION STARTERS

1. Before Otto or Louisa, Rolf emigrates to America. He seems to have a strong vision of the American Dream, and to associate it with the promise of the Western Frontier. In what ways do associated themes of liberation and adventure come to fruition in his life?

2. Discuss the power structure evidenced in Louisa's relationship with men over the course of her adolescence and adulthood. In what ways is she powerful or powerless in relation to these young men, notably Julian, Phillip, and Rolf?

3. Dr. Seidelbaum commits a near-fatal—and debilitating—error during surgery. Is there an underlying message here about the extent to which life can *or cannot* be controlled?

4. In World War I, Franz, Sigmund, and Emil—Louisa's, Rolf's, and Otto's fathers, respectively—received an Iron Cross for bravery. They are models of heroism. Do their progeny honor this memory? Do any of them evince heroism themselves, even if it takes a different form?

5. As a member of the refugee committee on which her husband serves, Louisa tries to minister to German Jews who are struggling to survive in New York. In one instance, she gives ribbon and a green bead necklace (p. 65), and in others, "lace doilies or French soap" (p. 109). Even if these gifts are frivolous, are Louisa's ministrations to be discounted?

6. In your view, is Mrs. Sprague manipulative or well intentioned? What does she do to convince you of either opinion?

7. Gustav and Sophie Joseftal argue about whether Rolf is being "cruel" or "just" to Louisa once she has become partially paralyzed (p. 171). Does Rolf's attempt to be just to her itself become a form of cruelty? Is it possible to be just and cruel at the same time? If so, how?

8. When Sophie Joseftal counsels Louisa to fire Mrs. Sprague over her controlling care of Emma, Louisa replies that "[Emma] has the right to her loves"—in other words, a right to her apparent preference for Mrs. Sprague (p. 189). How do you see this issue of "the right to love" at play within the novel?

9. What is the significance of the "Oriental wife" within the novel? In what ways do Louisa's and Emma's encounters with this persona reinforce or contradict one another?

The Paris Wife

By Paula McLain

Chicago, 1920: Hadley Richardson is a quiet twenty-eight-year-old who has all but given up on love and happiness—until she meets Ernest Hemingway and her life changes forever. Following a whirlwind courtship and wedding, the pair set sail for Paris, where they become the golden couple in a lively and volatile group. Though deeply in love, the Hemingways are ill prepared for the hard-drinking and fast-living life of Jazz Age Paris, which hardly values traditional notions of family and monogamy. Ernest struggles to find the voice that will earn him a place in history, pouring all the richness and intensity of his life with Hadley and their circle of friends into the novel that will become *The Sun Also Rises*. Hadley, meanwhile, strives to hold on to her sense of self as the demands of life with Ernest grow costly and her roles as wife, friend, and muse become more challenging. Despite their extraordinary bond, they eventually find themselves facing the ultimate crisis of their marriage.

A heartbreaking portrayal of love and torn loyalty, *The Paris Wife* is all the more poignant because we know that, in the end, Hemingway wrote that he would rather have died than fallen in love with anyone but Hadley.

"McLain smartly explores Hadley's ambivalence about her role as supportive wife to a budding genius. . . . Women and book groups are going to eat up this novel." —USA **Today**

ABOUT THE AUTHOR: **Paula McLain** was born in Fresno, California, in 1965. She received her MFA in poetry from the University of Michigan in 1996, and since then has been a resident at Yaddo and the recipient of fellowships from the National Endowment for the Arts. She is the author of two collections of poetry, a much-praised memoir, and one previous and well-received novel, *A Ticket to Ride*. Paula McLain lives in Cleveland, Ohio, with her family.

February 2011 | Hardcover | Fiction | 336 pp | $25.00 | ISBN 9780345521309
Ballantine Books | randomhouse.com
Also available as: eBook and Audiobook

CONVERSATION STARTERS

1. Hadley and Ernest don't get a lot of encouragement from their friends and family when they decided to marry. What seems to draw the two together? What are some of the strengths of their initial attraction and partnership?

2. Throughout *The Paris Wife*, Hadley refers to herself as "Victorian" as opposed to "modern." What are some of the ways she doesn't feel like she fits into life in bohemian Paris? How does this impact her relationship with Ernest? Her self-esteem?

3. Hadley and Ernest's marriage survived for many years in Jazz-Age Paris, an environment that had very little patience for monogamy and other traditional values. What in their relationship seems to sustain them?

4. One of the most wrenching scenes in the book is when Hadley loses a valise containing all of Ernest's work to date. What kind of turning point does this mark for the Hemingway's marriage? Do you think Ernest ever forgives her?

5. In *The Paris Wife* , when Ernest receives his contract for *In Our Time*, Hadley says, "He would never again be unknown. We would never again be this happy." How did fame affect Ernest and his relationship with Hadley?

6. *The Sun Also Rises* is drawn from the Hemingways' real-life experiences with bullfighting in Spain. Ernest and his friends are clearly present in the book, but Hadley is not. Why? In what ways do you think Hadley is instrumental to the book regardless?

7. What was the nature of the relationship between Hadley and Pauline Pfeiffer? Were they legitimately friends? How do you see Pauline taking advantage of her intimate position in the Hemingway's life? Do you think Hadley is naïve for not suspecting Pauline of having designs on Ernest earlier? Why or why not?

8. What would it have cost for Hadley to stick it out with Ernest no matter what? Is there a way she could have fought harder for her marriage?

9. When Hemingway's biographer Carlos Baker interviewed Hadley Richardson near the end of her life, he expected her to be bitter, and yet she persisted in describing Ernest as a "prince." How can she have continued to love and admire him after the way he hurt her?

10. Ernest Hemingway spent the last months of his life tenderly reliving his first marriage in the pages his memoir, *A Moveable Feast*. In fact, it was the last thing he wrote before his death. Do you think he realized what he'd truly lost with Hadley?

The Particular Sadness of Lemon Cake

By Aimee Bender

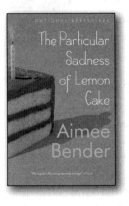

On the eve of her ninth birthday, unassuming Rose Edelstein, a girl at the periphery of schoolyard games and her distracted parents' attention, bites into her mother's homemade lemon-chocolate cake and discovers she has a magical gift: she can taste her mother's emotions in the cake. She discovers this gift to her horror, for her mother—her cheerful, good-with-crafts, can-do mother—tastes of despair and desperation. Suddenly, and for the rest of her life, food becomes a peril and a threat to Rose.

The curse her gift has bestowed is the secret knowledge all families keep hidden—her mother's life outside the home, her father's detachment, her brother's clash with the world. Yet as Rose grows up she learns to harness her gift and becomes aware that there are secrets even her taste buds cannot discern.

*"Moving, fanciful, and gorgeously strange." —**People***

*"Marvelous. . . . Few writers are as adept as Bender at mingling magical elements so seamlessly with the ordinary." —**San Francisco Chronicle***

*"A richly imagined, bittersweet tale." —**Vanity Fair***

ABOUT THE AUTHOR: **Aimee Bender** is the author of four books: *The Girl in the Flammable Skirt, An Invisible Sign of My Own, Willful Creatures,* and *The Particular Sadness of Lemon Cake* (2010), which recently won the SCIBA award for best fiction and an Alex Award. Her short fiction has been published in *Granta, GQ, Harper's, Tin House, McSweeney's,* and *The Paris Review.* She has received two Pushcart prizes, and was nominated for the TipTree award in 2005, and the Shirley Jackson short story award in 2010. Her fiction has been translated into sixteen languages. She lives in Los Angeles, where she teaches creative writing at USC.

April 2011 | Trade Paperback | Fiction | 304 pp | $15.00 | ISBN 9780385720960
Anchor | readinggroupcenter.com | flammableskirt.com
Also available as: eBook and Audiobook

CONVERSATION STARTERS

1. Rose goes through life feeling people's emotions through their food. Many eat to feel happy and comforted. Does this extreme sensory experience bring any happiness to Rose or only sadness?

2. What does Rose mean when she says her dad always seemed like a guest to her? How does this play out in the rest of the novel?

3. "Mom's smiles were so full of feeling that people leaned back a little when she greeted them. It was hard to know just how much was being offered." What does Rose mean and how does this trait affect her mother's relationships?

4. Why do you think Rose's dad liked medical dramas but hated hospitals?

5. Rose says, "Mom loved my brother more. Not that she didn't love me—I felt the wash of her love everyday, pouring over me, but it was a different kind, siphoned from a different, and tamer, body of water. I was her darling daughter; Joseph was her it." Do you think Rose is right in her estimation and why do you think her mother might feel this way?

6. What does the grandmother suggest when she tells Rose "you don't even know me, how can you love me?" How has the grandmother's relationship with Rose's own mother affected the family dynamic?

7. What is Joseph trying to accomplish by drawing a "perfect" circle when it, by very definition, is impossible? How does George's idea to create wallpaper out of the imperfections affect him?

8. Why does George suddenly conclude Rose's gift isn't really a problem and stops investigating it?

9. What is the significance of the mother's commitment to carpentry (compared to other, short-lived hobbies)? How does this play out in the rest of the novel?

10. What is the impact of Rose's discovery about her father's skills? Did this change the way you see the father?

11. Joseph is described as a desert and geode while Rose is a rainforest and sea glass. Discuss the implications.

12. Why does Rose want to keep the thread-bare footstool of her parents' courtship instead of having her mother make her a new one?

13. How did you experience the scene in Joseph's room, when Rose goes to see him? What did that experience mean to Rose? Is there any significance to Joseph choosing a card table chair?

14. What does the last image about the trees have to do with this family? How do you interpret the last line of the novel?

Picking Bones from Ash

By Marie Mutsuki Mockett

No one knows who fathered eleven-year-old Satomi, and the women of her 1950s Japanese mountain town find her mother's restless sensuality a threat. Satomi's success in piano competitions has always won respect, saving her and her mother from complete ostracism. But when her mother's growing ambition tests this delicate social balance, Satomi's gift is not enough to protect them. Eventually, Satomi is pushed to make a drastic decision in order to begin her life anew. Years later, Satomi's choices echo in the life of her American daughter, Rumi, a gifted authenticator of Asian antiques. Rumi has always believed her mother to be dead, but when Rumi begins to see a ghost, she wonders: Is this the spirit of her mother? If so, what happened to Satomi?

Picking Bones from Ash explores the struggles women face in accepting their talents, and asks what happens when mothers and daughters dare to question the debt owed each other. Fusing imagination and suspense, Marie Mutsuki Mockett builds a lavish world in which characters journey from Buddhist temples to the black market of international antiques in California, as they struggle to understand each other across cultures and generations.

"A book of intelligence and heart. As Mockett reveals, the ghosts of our mothers are always within us." —**Amy Tan**

ABOUT THE AUTHOR: **Marie Mutsuki Mockett** was born in Carmel, California, to a Japanese mother and an American father. She is a graduate of Columbia University with a degree in East Asian studies. Mockett's essay "Letter from a Japanese Crematorium" was cited as a notable in *Best American Essays 2008*. She has been a Bernard O'Keefe Scholar for Nonfiction at the Bread Loaf Writers' Conference. *Picking Bones from Ash* was shortlisted for the Saroyan International Prize, a finalist for the Paterson Prize, and longlisted for the Asian American Literary Awards. She lives with her Scottish husband and son in New York City. *Picking Bones from Ash* is her first novel.

February 2011 | Trade Paperback | Fiction | 320 pp | $15.00 | ISBN 9781555975760
Graywolf Press | graywolfpress.org | mariemockett.com
Also available as: eBook

CONVERSATION STARTERS

1. At the beginning of the book, Satomi says: "My mother always told me there is only one way a woman can be truly safe in this world. And that is to be fiercely, inarguably, and masterfully talented." Is Satomi safe in the end? At what cost? And what about the other female characters, particularly Akiko and Rumi? What does it mean for a woman to be safe?

2. Satomi seeks out Western music in Paris, Timothy yearns for spiritual enlightenment through Buddhism, and François reinvents himself in San Francisco. Discuss the ways in which these and other characters—and perhaps you yourself—find freedom through other cultures, and comfort in what is native.

3. On page 246, Satomi tells Rumi, "Here we are. A girl without a mother and a girl with too much of a mother. Which, I wonder, would most people rather be? One inherits history. The other is free to create it herself." Do you think it is better to inherit history or to create a history for yourself?

4. François teaches Rumi the importance of seeing beauty out of context. How does this skill help her later on? How does it relate to the Buddhist notion of seeing through illusion?

5. Why do you think the ghost of Akiko revealed itself to Rumi and not to Satomi?

6. Masayoshi says: "When parents and children can accept each other—no matter what that means—their relationships with everyone else will change" (page 272). How do you feel about this statement?

7. Mockett has said: "I felt it was important that any supernatural elements in my novel would be grounded in psychological truths, because that's the 'reality' of true supernatural experiences." How does the supernatural function within her story? Does it add atmosphere? Did it detract from the story?

8. On page 224, Akira says: "The world of the living can be like that of the dead. It is tragic when we lose ourselves in grief." What do you think about this statement? Is it something that you or someone close to you has experienced?

9. At the end of the novel, Akiko says to Satomi: "You look like a loved person. It always shows on people's faces. The ones who discover love when they are much older always look startled." Do you agree?

Pictures of You

By Caroline Leavitt

Two women running away from their marriages collide on a foggy highway, killing one of them. The survivor, Isabelle, is left to pick up the pieces, not only of her own life, but of the lives of the devastated husband and fragile son that the other woman, April, has left behind. Together, they try to solve the mystery of where April was running to, and why. As these three lives intersect, the book asks, how well do we really know those we love—and how do we forgive the unforgivable?

"A beautiful book—about the mistakes we make and how we redeem ourselves in the wake of a tragedy. . . . Leavitt writes with a really light and delicate touch about the relationships between people. She's an undiscovered jewel." —**Jodi Picoult, Newsweek**

"Leavitt is superb at revealing the secrecy inside many marriages and the way children grieve. . . . Most impressive is how Leavitt deals head-on with well-meaning people who come to realize, too late, that even an imperfect life is irreplaceable." —**O: The Oprah Magazine**

"Vivid descriptions and passages of striking insight and wrenching, visceral power. . . . Leavitt beautifully paces the book's intertwining stories, meticulously unfurling bits of the back story, letting us put together the pieces." —**Boston Globe**

ABOUT THE AUTHOR: **Caroline Leavitt** is the award-winning author of eight novels. Her essays and stories have been included in *New York Magazine, Psychology Today, More, Parenting, Redbook,* and *Salon.* She's a columnist for the *Boston Globe,* a book reviewer for *People,* and a writing instructor at UCLA online. Leavitt lives in Hoboken, New Jersey, New York City's unofficial sixth borough, with her husband, the writer Jeff Tamarkin, and their teenage son Max.

January 2011 | Trade Paperback| Fiction | 336 pp | $13.95 | ISBN 9781565126312
Algonquin Books | algonquinbooks.com | carolineleavitt.com
Also available as: eBook and Audiobook

CONVERSATION STARTERS

1. Pulitzer Prize winner Robert Olen Butler commented that Leavitt's book is about "how each of us tries to shape our deepest sense of self, challenged not only by other souls in similar pursuit, but by the very forces of life itself." How do you see this played out in *Pictures of You* or in your own life?

2. Sam's asthma impacts his life, April's and Charlie's. At one point, on page 64, April tells Charlie that she heard that "breathing is our contract to stay on this planet." If this is so, why do you think that Sam's asthma vanishes? What made Sam want to stay on earth and survive?

3. Early in the novel, Sam remembers how he and his mother used to go on short trips and pretend to be other people with other lives. Why do you think people need to create different realities for themselves? What function can it serve and how can it be both helpful and harmful?

4. As Isabelle teaches Sam about photography, she explains that photographs sometimes show things that aren't there. She tells him that he has to learn to look deeper, and in a way, she's really talking about people, as well as photographs. How much do you think we can ever really know about the people we love?

5. Leavitt's book explores the many different kinds of love: Why do you think Isabelle's love for her tortoise figures so prominently in the novel? Why do you think Isabelle fell in love with a tortoise, rather than a dog or a cat?

6. Why do you think Leavitt chose to flash forward thirty years and show Sam as an adult? Was Sam's life what you expected it might be or were you surprised by his choices?

7. Leavitt has said that the novel is about the stories we tell ourselves about the ones we love. How do the stories keep each person from truly seeing the one they love?

8. The novel asks, can we forgive the unforgivable? Do you think Charlie ever really forgives April? Do you?

9. What do you think the title, *Pictures of You*, really refers to?

10. Leavitt has said that she wanted to create a never-ending story that would make readers wonder about the characters long after they turned the last page. What do you think happens to Sam? Do you think Charlie and Isabelle ever meet again?

Please Look After Mom

By Kyung-Sook Shin

A million-plus-copy best seller in Korea—a magnificent English-language debut poised to become an international sensation—this is the stunning, deeply moving story of a family's search for their mother, who goes missing one afternoon amid the crowds of the Seoul Station subway.

Told through the piercing voices and urgent perspectives of a daughter, son, husband, and mother, *Please Look After Mom* is at once an authentic picture of contemporary life in Korea and a universal story of family love.

You will never think of your mother the same way again after you read this book.

"A raw tribute to the mysteries of motherhood. . . . Shin's prose, intimate, and hauntingly spare, powerfully conveys grief's bewildering immediacy." **—The New York Times Book Review**

"A suspenseful, haunting, achingly lovely novel about the hidden lives, wishes, struggles and dreams of those we think we know best." **—Seattle Times**

"Titles to Pick Up Now: This best-seller set in the author's native Korea examines a family's history through the story of the matriarch, mysteriously gone missing from a Seoul train station." **—Karen Holt, O, the Oprah Magazine**

ABOUT THE AUTHOR: **Kyung-Sook Shin** is the author of numerous works of fiction and is one of South Korea's most widely read and acclaimed novelists. She has been honored with the Manhae Literature Prize, the Dong-in Literature Prize, and the Yi Sang Literary Prize, as well as France's Prix de l'Inaperçu. *Please Look After Mom* is her first book to appear in English and will be published in nineteen countries. Shin is currently a visiting scholar at Columbia University in New York City. She lives in Seoul.

April 2012 | Trade Paperback | Fiction | $14.95 | ISBN 9780307739513
Vintage | readinggroupcenter.com
Also available as: eBook and Audiobook

CONVERSATION STARTERS

1. While second-person ("you") narration is an uncommon mode, it is used throughout the novel's first section (the tale of the daughter, Chi-hon) and third section (the tale of the husband). What is the effect of this choice? How does it reflect these characters' feelings about Mom? Why do you think Mom is the only character who tells her story in the first person?

2. What do we learn about the relationship between Chi-hon and her mother? What are the particular sources of tension or resentment between them? Why does Chi-hon say to her brother, "Maybe I'm being punished . . ."?

3. What are some of the reasons for the special bond between the eldest son, Hyong-chol, and his mother?

4. Why does Hyong-chol feel that he has disappointed his mother? Why does she apologize to him when she brings Chi-hon to live with him? Why do you think he hasn't achieved his goals?

5. The Full Moon Harvest is a festival in which Koreans traditionally return to their family home to honor their ancestors. Hyong-chol reflects that people are now beginning to take holidays out of the country instead, saying, "Ancestors, I'll be back." What feelings do memories of their mother's preparations for the festival stir up in Chi-hon, Hyong-chol, and their father?

6. Weeks after his wife disappears, her husband discovers that for ten years she has been giving a substantial amount of money—money their children send her each month—to an orphanage where she has taken on many responsibilities. How does the husband react to this and other surprising discoveries about her life?

7. Discuss the return of Mom as storyteller and narrator in the fourth section. What is inventive about this choice on the author's part? What surprised you—and what remained a mystery?

8. What are we to understand of the fact of Mom's possibly being spotted, in chapter 2, in the various neighborhoods where Hyong-chol has lived in Seoul? In Mom's own narrative, what is the connection between herself and the bird her daughter sees "sitting on the quince tree"?

9. What are the details and cultural references that make this story particularly Korean? What elements make it universal?

Prayers and Lies

By Sherri Wood Emmons

When seven-year-old Bethany meets her six-year-old cousin Reana Mae, it's the beginning of a kinship of misfits that saves both from a bone-deep loneliness. Every summer, Bethany and her family leave Indianapolis for West Virginia's Coal River Valley. For Bethany's mother, the trips are a reminder of the coalmines and grinding poverty of her childhood, of a place she'd hoped to escape. But her loving relatives, and Bethany's friendship with Reana Mae, keep them coming back.

But as Bethany grows older, she realizes that life in this small, close-knit community is not as simple as she once thought . . . that the riverside cabins that hold so much of her family's history also teem with scandalous whispers . . . and that those closest to her harbor unimaginable secrets. Amid the dense woods and quiet beauty of the valley, these secrets are coming to light at last, with a force devastating enough to shatter lives, faith, and the bond that Bethany once thought would last forever.

Spanning four decades, Sherri Wood Emmons' debut is a haunting, captivating novel about the unexpected, sometimes shocking events that thrust us into adulthood—and the connections that keep us tethered, always, to our pasts.

"Emmons perfectly captures the devastating impact of family secrets in her beautifully written—and ultimately hopeful—debut novel. A must read."
—**Diane Chamberlain, author of *The Lies We Told***

ABOUT THE AUTHOR: **Sherri Wood Emmons** is a freelance writer and editor. *Prayers and Lies* is her first work of fiction. She is a graduate of Earlham College and the University of Denver Publishing Institute. A mother of three, she lives in Indiana with her husband, two fat beagles, and four spoiled cats.

January 2011 | Trade Paperback | Fiction | 320 pp | $15.00 | ISBN 9780758253248
Kensington Books | kensingtonbooks.com | sherriwoodemmons.com
Also available as: eBook and Audiobook

CONVERSATION STARTERS

1. Is there a villain in the story? Who is the villain? Is there anything that makes his or her actions understandable? Is that character redeemable?

2. Aunt Belle explains to Reana Mae and Bethany that Helen's family carries "bad blood." What is the bad blood? How might it be diagnosed today?

3. Does knowing about the bad blood change the way you view Tracy?

4. Do Helen and Jimmy bear responsibility for Tracy's death? What could they have done to prevent it?

5. Did Jolene have a right to know who her father was? Should Helen have told her? Why or why not?

6. Is there any good in the relationship between Reana Mae and Caleb? What good would that be?

7. Why did Reana Mae have sex with Harley Boy on the day of Araminta's funeral? What does her decision say about her attitude toward sex?

8. How might the story have changed if Jolene had not lost her baby?

9. What responsibility does Bobby Lee bear for Reana Mae's relationship with Caleb?

10. Were Harley Boy, Ruthanne, and Bethany right to keep quiet after they found out about Reana Mae and Caleb? Should they have told their parents the truth?

11. What role does Neil play in the story?

12. Why is the book titled *Prayers and Lies*? Is there a faith element to the story?

13. Why is the story told from Bethany's perspective? Is that an effective narrative device? How might the story be different if it was told in the third person?

14. Was moving Reana Mae to Indianapolis the right decision for her? Was it the right decision for the rest of the family?

15. What enabled Helen to rise above the circumstances of her childhood and become a sane, loving mother?

16. Given the family history of "bad blood," is it irresponsible for Bethany to choose to have a child?

Q: A Novel

By Evan Mandery

Shortly before his wedding, the unnamed hero of this uncommon romance is visited by a man who claims to be his future self and ominously admonishes him that he must not marry the love of his life, Q. At first the protagonist doubts this stranger, but in time he becomes convinced of the authenticity of the warning and leaves his fiancée. The resulting void in his life is impossible to fill. One after the other, future selves arrive urging him to marry someone else, divorce, attend law school, leave law school, travel, join a running club, stop running, study the guitar, the cello, Proust, Buddhism, and opera, and eliminate gluten from his diet. The only constants in this madcap quest for personal improvement are his love for his New York City home and for the irresistible Q.

A unique literary talent, Evan Mandery turns the classic story of transcendent love on its head. Mandery brilliantly blends outrageous humor, existential philosophy, and heartbreaking angst while offering a wealth of satisfying surprises. Funny and wise, *Q: A Novel* is a magical tale of a man obsessed yet unable to allow himself the fulfillment of a perfect romance with the one true love of his life.

"A philosophical, witty, wonderful and altogether magical love story. Existential questions have never been couched in a more tender way."
—**M.J. Rose, author of** *The Hypnotist*

ABOUT THE AUTHOR: **Evan Mandery** is a graduate of Harvard Law School, a professor at John Jay College of Criminal Justice in New York City, and the author of two works each of fiction and nonfiction.

September 2011 | Trade Paperback | Fiction | 368 pp | $13.99 | ISBN 9780062015839
Harper Paperbacks | harpercollins.com | evanmandery.com
Also available as: eBook

CONVERSATION STARTERS

1. *Q* raises some important moral questions. Was it ethical for the older version of the main character, I-55, to encourage the main character to change the path of his life? What about the other older versions?

2. Relatedly, and perhaps most importantly, was it ethical for the main character to decide to abandon Q? Did Q have a right to know the basis for his decision?

3. Are the main character and the future versions of himself the same people? If not, what implications does this have for how we think of ourselves? Is a ten-year old version of myself the same person as me? A thirty-year older version? Fifty?

4. In *Q*, the price of time travel is extremely high. Does it matter whether a new technology is egalitarian, meaning that it is accessible to all people? Would time travel, on the terms discussed in *Q*, be an improvement to society?

5. The debate between Herbert Spencer and Sigmund Freud in Chapter 18 is central to the theme of the book. All of the future versions of the main character believe they are making the main character's life better. Is this belief in progress real or is faux-Freud correct in saying that it is something humans have created to make their lives palatable?

6. Is Q's father a believable character? Is it possible that he is a different person with Q than in his business dealings?

7. The author writes the entire book in present tense. What do you think of this as a literary technique? What, if anything, is the author's message in making this choice?

8. *Q* is a comedy with a supremely tragic premise. Are these choices compatible or incompatible?

9. If you could visit yourself at an earlier point, where would you go and what, if anything, would you say?

10. If you could visit another place and time, where and when would you go?

Reading Women
How the Great Books of Feminism Changed My Life
By Stephanie Staal

When Stephanie Staal first read *The Feminine Mystique* in college, she found it "a mildly interesting relic from another era." But more than a decade later, as a married stay-at-home mom in the suburbs, Staal rediscovered Betty Friedan's classic work—and was surprised how much she identified with the laments and misgivings of 1950s housewives. She set out on a quest: to reenroll at Barnard and re-read the great books she had first encountered as an undergrad.

From the banishment of Eve to Judith Butler's *Gender Trouble*, Staal explores the significance of each of these classic tales by and of women, highlighting the relevance these ideas still have today. This process leads Staal to find the self she thought she had lost—curious and ambitious, zany and critical—and inspires new understandings of her relationships with her husband, her mother, and her daughter

"[A] brave and compelling book. . . . I cherished every page." —**J. Courtney Sullivan, author of *Commencement* and *Maine***

"Reading Women is terrific. Stephanie Staal's exploration of the great texts of the women who have walked before us is fresh, funny, and a wise reminder that now, more than ever, we need to feed the feminist within." —**Katie Crouch, author of *New York Times* bestselling *Girls in Trucks***

ABOUT THE AUTHOR: **Stephanie Staal** is a former features reporter for the *Newark Star-Ledger*, and has written for *Cosmopolitan, Glamour, Self*, and the *Washington Post*. She is the author of *The Love They Lost*, a journalistic memoir about the long-term effects of parental divorce. A graduate of Barnard College and Columbia University's Graduate School of Journalism, she recently received her J.D. from Brooklyn Law School. Staal lives in Brooklyn, New York.

February 2011 | Trade Paperback | Memoir | 394 pp | $15.99 | ISBN 9781586488727
PublicAffairs | publicaffairsbooks.com | stephaniestaal.com
Also available as: eBook

CONVERSATION STARTERS

1. What did you think of the author's decision to return to Barnard and take Feminist Texts? If you could go back to college and re-take one course, which one would it be?

2. Have you read any of the books from the Feminist Texts syllabus? Which one has made a mark on your life?

3. Staal writes a lot about the work/mother dichotomy, and how difficult it is for women everywhere to inhabit these roles fully simultaneously. If you are a parent, how have you handled this situation?

4. At a panel the author attends, one of the panelists says "Well I don't know if we should tell our daughters that they have *limitless* possibilities." Do you think it's disingenuous to tell our daughters that they can "have it all?"

5. The class encounters different types of feminists throughout the course of their readings—from the radical feminists like Shulamith Firestone to the "post-feminists" like Katie Roiphe. How do you define a feminist? Do you consider yourself a feminist? If you do consider yourself a feminist, can you attribute it to a particular event or experience in your life?

6. The last text Staal reads for her class is a blog called "Baghdad Burning." What non-canonical texts—whether it be fiction, non-fiction, poetry, blog, book, magazine or other types of writing—have contributed most to your understanding of feminism?

7. Staal observes many differences between opinions she espoused while in college and those of her Generation Y classmates. How do you think the younger generation, raised in the social network/Facebook era, will respond differently to the challenges of reconciling adulthood or motherhood with feminism? Will it be any easier for them than it was for the author's generation?

8. Staal is upset by the *New York Times* article about Ivy League women opting out of the workforce "not so much because these young women wanted to be stay-at-home mothers, but for their seeming readiness, at nineteen years old, to resort to traditional gender roles without a peep." What do you think of that article? Of Staal's opinion?

9. Of all of the books the author writes about, which one intrigued you the most? Which author was the most interesting to you?

Rivals in the Tudor Court

By D. L. Bogdan

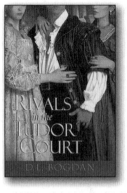

As Queen Catherine's maid and daughter of the Duke of Buckingham, the future seems bright for Elizabeth Stafford. But when her father gives her hand to Thomas Howard, third Duke of Norfolk, the spirited young woman must sacrifice all for duty. Yet Elizabeth is surprised by her passion for her powerful new husband. And when he takes on a mistress, she is determined to fight for her love and her honor. Naïve and vulnerable, Bess Holland is easily charmed by the Duke of Norfolk, doing his bidding in exchange for gifts and adoration. For years, she and Elizabeth compete for his affections. But they are mere spectators to an obsession neither can rival: Norfolk's quest to weave the Howard name into the royal bloodline. The women's loyalties are tested as his schemes unfold—among them the litigious marriage of his niece, Anne Boleyn, to King Henry the VIII. But in an age of ruthless beheadings, no self-serving motive goes unpunished—and Elizabeth and Bess will have to fight a force more sinister than the executioner's axe.

"Throbs with intensity as it lays bare the secret delights of Tudor court life and the sudden, lethal terrors." —**Barbara Kyle, author of *The King's Daughter* on *Secrets of the Tudor Court***

ABOUT THE AUTHOR: **D. L. Bogdan** is a history major, aiming for a master's so that she might lecture one day. She is also a musician with classical voice training who has been playing keyboards and singing in bands since she was 18. She also enjoys reading, traveling, summer activities, spending time with family and friends, and researching her next novel! She makes her home in central Wisconsin.

April 2011 | Trade Paperback | Fiction | 352 pp | $15.00 | ISBN 9780758242006
Kensington Books | kensingtonbooks.com | dlbogdan.com
Also available as: eBook

CONVERSATION STARTERS

1. Explain Thomas Howard's descent of character. What were the key factors in his life that contributed to his moral and spiritual decline? Did he ever redeem himself?

2. Is there anything in this novel that supports the theory of nature vs. nurture? Was Thomas' nature predetermined genetically or was a he solely a product of his environment?

3. Elizabeth, as a sufferer of domestic violence, was ahead of her time in that she reached out to several sources for help, including Privy Seal Cromwell. Was she a heroine or a victim? Did she have any real allies?

4. Catherine of Aragon seemed to be a consistent source of contention in Thomas and Elizabeth's marriage. Compare and contrast Elizabeth and Thomas' relationship with this formidable woman.

5. Throughout the story, Thomas and Elizabeth's relationship undergoes many changes. Note the turning points in their marriage. Did they love each other?

6. Compare and contrast Thomas' attitude before and after he attained the title Duke of Norfolk.

7. Bess Holland's position as mistress and servant is not an unusual one for the times. Why did she stay? Did she love Thomas?

8. Bess also undergoes changes in character throughout the novel. Did she become stronger or weaker?

9. Did the women in this story, Bess, Elizabeth, and Mary Howard, do the right thing by testifying against Thomas at his trial?

10. The novel focuses on some mystical elements, touching on reincarnation in the subplot involving Princess Anne Plantagenet and Norfolk's daughter Mary Howard. Do you believe in reincarnation? Why do you think the author chose to portray this subplot this way?

11. Compare and contrast Thomas' relationship with his first wife and family as opposed to his second.

12. Did Thomas love Henry VIII or was he simply a channel for his ambition?

13. Did Thomas' time in the Tower change him in any fundamental ways?

14. Did Thomas and Elizabeth find forgiveness for each other by novel's end or was it a merely a deathbed truce?

15. What is the relevance of Thomas' signet ring for him, Elizabeth, and Bess?

Russian Winter

By Daphne Kalotay

When she decides to auction her remarkable jewelry collection, Nina Revskaya, once a great star of the Bolshoi ballet, believes she has drawn a curtain on her past. Instead, the aged dancer finds herself overwhelmed by memories of her homeland and of the events—both glorious and heartbreaking—that changed the course of her life half a century before.

It was in Russia that she discovered the magic of the theatre; that she fell in love with the poet Viktor Elsin; that she and her dearest companions—Gersh, a dangerously irreverent composer, and the exquisite Vera, Nina's closest friend—became victims of Stalinist aggression; that a terrible discovery led to a deadly act of betrayal—and to an ingenious escape that eventually brought her to the city of Boston.

Nina has hidden her dark secrets for half a lifetime. But two people will not let the past rest—Drew Brooks, an inquisitive young associate director at the Boston auction house, and a Russian professor named Grigori Solodin who believes that a unique set of amber jewels may hold the key to his own ambiguous past. Together, these unlikely partners find themselves unraveling a literary mystery whose answers will hold life-changing consequences for them all.

"An auspicious first novel, elegantly written and without a false note."
—*Kirkus Reviews* (starred review)

ABOUT THE AUTHOR: **Daphne Kalotay**, the author of the acclaimed fiction collection *Calamity and Other Stories*, attended Boston University's Creative Writing Program before going on to complete a literature PhD. She has been a fellow of the Christopher Isherwood Foundation, Yaddo, and the MacDowell Colony as well as a recipient of the Rose Fellowship in the Creative Arts from Vassar College. She has taught creative writing at Boston University, Middlebury College, and Skidmore College, and lives in the Boston area.

April 2011 | Trade Paperback | Fiction | 498 pp | $14.99 | ISBN 9780061962172
Harper Perennial | harpercollins.com | daphnekalotay.com
Also available as: eBook and Audiobook

CONVERSATION STARTERS

1. How would you describe Nina Revskaya? What kind a person was she? Do you sympathize with the way events shaped the woman she became? And how would you compare her with Vera Borodina? What held them back from sharing their deepest secrets?

2. Each piece of Nina's jewelry denotes a particular memory. Why do you think she waited so long to finally part with her jewels? Are there memories we have that are too painful to face, yet too dear to let go of? Do any of your possessions hold a special memory for you?

3. In your opinion, did Viktor Elsin truly love Nina? Did she love him? What about Gersh and Vera? What sacrifices were each willing to make for love?

4. After she defected, Nina believed she had shed the first third of her life. To what extent was this true? Can we ever truly rid ourselves of parts of our lives—or ourselves—that we don't like?

5. Nina cherished the solitude of her later years. Was her solitude a release, or was it a fortress she used to keep others—and the past—away?

6. Was Nina a victim of the society in which she was raised—or a perpetrator of its worst abuses? Would her ambitions have eventually led her to behave the way her jealousy ultimately caused her to act?

7. Were Gersh, Viktor and Vera radicals? What makes someone a dissident? Why do nations like the former Soviet Union insist on silencing all criticism?

8. What did art—the ballet—mean to Nina? Did she have to make a choice between dance and love? Could she have balanced both? What about women today?

9. Zoltan, also a refugee from the Iron Curtain, tells Grigori, "I remember before I left Hungary understanding completely that literature could save me as much as it could get me killed. Of course it's not like that here. But isn't it funny, that in some ways the price one pays for freedom of speech is . . . a kind of indifference." What does he mean by this? Must an artist suffer in some way to produce art?

10. "Even when she tried to will it open, Nina's heart would not budge." Why couldn't she open herself up to new love and new friends? What held her back—habit, or guilt?

11. Have you ever met anyone who has lived under repressive circumstances? How did discovering their story affect you or your outlook?

The Sandalwood Tree

By Elle Newmark

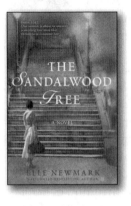

From incredible storyteller and nationally bestselling author Elle Newmark comes a rich, sweeping novel that brings to life two love stories, ninety years apart, set against the backdrop of war-torn India.

In 1947, an American anthropologist named Martin Mitchell wins a Fulbright Fellowship to study in India. He travels there with his wife, Evie, and his son, determined to start a new chapter in their lives. Upon the family's arrival, though, they are forced to stay in a small village due to violence surrounding Britain's imminent departure from India. It is there, hidden behind a brick wall in their colonial bungalow, that Evie discovers a packet of old letters that tell a strange and compelling story of love and war involving two young Englishwomen who lived in the very same house in 1857.

Drawn to their story, Evie embarks on a mission to uncover what the letters didn't explain. Her search leads her through the bazaars and temples of India as well as the dying society of the British Raj. Along the way, a dark secret is exposed, and this new and disturbing knowledge creates a wedge between Evie and her husband. Bursting with lavish detail and vivid imagery of Bombay and beyond, *The Sandalwood Tree* is a powerful story about betrayal, forgiveness, fate, and love.

"Elle Newmark beautifully captures the sights, smells and sounds of India on the cusp of change, all the while spinning a richly layered tale."
—**Cathy Buchanan, New York Times bestselling author of *The Day the Falls Stood Still***

ABOUT THE AUTHOR: **Elle Newmark** is the acclaimed author of *The Book of Unholy Mischief.* She lived and worked in the hills north of San Diego.

March 2012 | Trade Paperback | Fiction | 368 pp | $15.00 | ISBN 9781416590606
Atria | imprints.simonandschuster.biz/atria | ellenewmark.com
Also available as: eBook

CONVERSATION STARTERS

1. *The Sandalwood Tree* begins with a quote from Adela Winfield: "[D]eath steals everything but our stories." Later Evie paraphrases this as "[A]ll we really have are our stories" (p. 330) What do you think of this? Do you agree? Do you think our stories are the only things that last?

2. The British characters often mock the Indians' superstitions throughout the novel. Is Evie's need for order a superstition in itself? Do you think there's a difference between her need for order and the natives' need for their rituals? Are they driven by the same impulses and desires?

3. Felicity and Adela live in a time where a woman had very few choices, and society had very specific expectations of them. In spite of these, they manage to carve out nontraditional lives, vowing to "scrap the rules and live a life of joy, no matter what the price." (p. 28) What do you think makes them different from the other women of the era, able to make these choices?

4. Throughout *The Sandalwood Tree* there is a huge dichotomy between the rich foreigners, with their servants and extravagance, and the abject poverty of so many of the natives. Did this disparity bother you? Do you think it's inevitable that there be such a difference between classes?

5. The love affairs in the novel were all scandalous for their time: the interracial relationship between Jonathan Singh and Felicity, Adela's lesbian relationship, Martin and Evie's interfaith marriage. What does it say about the characters that they were all able to defy expectations and conventions? Did you find their decisions shocking?

6. Evie refers to India as "a spiritual carnival complete with sideshows." (pp. 111–112) The religious practices, divisions, and biases of the characters are a major theme in *The Sandalwood Tree*. Do you think it's possible for conflicting faiths to live in harmony, or is the war in the name of religion that plagues human history inescapable?

7. Martin cannot forgive himself for the things he did, and didn't do, during wartime. It is not until he tells Evie what happened, and she forgives him, that he can begin to forgive himself. Do you think Martin would be able to find any peace with his memories if he hadn't shared them with Evie? Or do you think it's only by not holding on to secrets that people can begin to get over them?

8. Harry quotes Gandhi as saying, "Poverty is the worst form of violence." What do you think of this statement?

Secret Daughter

By Shilpi Somaya Gowda

Somer's life is everything she imagined it would be—she's newly married and has started her career as a physician in San Francisco—until she makes the devastating discovery she never will be able to have children.

The same year in India, a poor mother makes the heartbreaking choice to save her newborn daughter's life by giving her away. It is a decision that will haunt Kavita for the rest of her life, and cause a ripple effect that travels across the world and back again.

Asha, adopted out of a Mumbai orphanage, is the child that binds the destinies of these two women. We follow both families, invisibly connected until Asha's journey of self-discovery leads her back to India.

Compulsively readable and deeply touching, *Secret Daughter* is a story of the unforeseen ways in which our choices and families affect our lives, and the indelible power of love in all its many forms

"[A] deeply moving and timeless story of an adopted daughter's long distance search for cultural identity and acceptance." —**Kathleen Kent, author of national bestseller *The Heretic's Daughter***

"Fiction with a conscience, as two couples worlds apart are linked by an adopted child. . . . A lightweight fable of family division and reconciliation, gaining intensity and depth from the author's sharp social observations" —***Kirkus***

About the Author: **Shilpi Somaya Gowda** was born and raised in Toronto to parents who migrated there from Mumbai. She holds an MBA from Stanford University, and a Bachelor's Degree from the University of North Carolina at Chapel Hill. In 1991, she spent a summer as a volunteer in an Indian orphanage. A native of Canada, she has lived in New York, North Carolina, and Texas. She now lives in California with her husband and children. Find Shilpi on Facebook.

April 2011 | Trade Paperback | Fiction | 386 pp | $13.99 | ISBN 9780061928352
William Morrow Paperbacks | harpercollins.com | shilpigowda.com
Also available as: eBook and Audiobook

CONVERSATION STARTERS

1. On the way to the orphanage in Bombay, Kavita reflects on "what power there is in naming another living being." What is the significance of these changing names throughout the story? How are names intertwined with your own sense of identity and belonging?

2. Kavita faces a difficult choice at the beginning of the novel. Did she make the right decision? What would you have done if you were in Kavita's place? What would the repercussions be of making a different choice?

3. Both families in the novel leave their home in search of better. Do you think their migrations were driven more by wanting to leave home or being attracted to a new place? Would the characters have made different choices if they knew what the consequences would be?

4. An overarching theme of the novel is motherhood, and how that experience can change a woman. Both Somer and Kavita have powerful experiences and emotions around pregnancy, childbirth and mothering. What are the differences in how they experience motherhood? Are there universal aspects to motherhood?

5. Both marriages portrayed in the novel, despite different circumstances and origins, face significant challenges. How did Kavita and Jasu's marriage recover from the dramatic conflict they faced at the beginning? What caused the estrangement between Krishnan and Somer? Do you believe one marriage is fundamentally stronger than the other? What do you believe the future holds for each couple?

6. Asha grows up with a deep curiosity about her biological family in India. Could her parents have done anything to lessen the sense of feeling incomplete Asha had as an adolescent? What does Asha learn about the true meaning of family, and could she have learned it without going to India?

7. This story turns on a twist of fate that changes the life path of Asha, and follows the parallel lives of Asha and her brother in India. Do you believe Asha was better off being taken to the orphanage as a baby than she would have been with her birth parents? How much of our lives are destined for us, and how much is within our power to change? Reflecting on your own life, what have been the turning points that have been made for you, and those made by you?

8. Were you surprised at the ending? How did your view of Jasu's character change from the beginning, and why? What do you imagine happens to these families next?

The Soldier's Wife

By Margaret Leroy

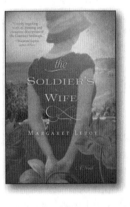

A novel full of grand passion and intensity, *The Soldier's Wife* asks "What would you do for your family?" "What should you do for a stranger?" and "What would you do for love?"

As World War II draws closer and closer to Guernsey, Vivienne de la Mare knows that there will be sacrifices to be made. Not just for herself, but for her two young daughters and for her mother-in-law, for whom she cares for while her husband is away fighting. What she does not expect is that she will fall in love with one of the enigmatic German soldiers who take up residence in the house next door to her home. As their relationship intensifies, so do the pressures on Vivienne. Food and resources grow scant, and the restrictions placed upon the residents of the island grow with each passing week. Though Vivienne knows the perils of her love affair with Gunther, she believes that she can keep their relationship—and her family—safe. But when she becomes aware of the full brutality of the Occupation, she must decide if she is willing to risk her personal happiness for the life of a stranger.

"Leroy lovingly portrays the era and the isolated Guernsey landscape while simultaneously offering an unsparing view of the specific horrors of war. Colourful, rich descriptions." —**Publishers Weekly**

"With its stunning and evocative description of the Guernsey landscape, its subtle and astute depiction of a woman's relationship with her children, her lover, and her husband, this absorbing novel is utterly beguiling."
—**Rosamund Lupton, author of *Sister***

ABOUT THE AUTHOR: **Margaret Leroy** has written five previous novels, including *Postcards from Berlin* (a *New York Times* Notable Book) and *Yes, My Darling Daughter*, which was chosen for the Oprah Summer Reading List. She is married with two children and lives in London.

June 2011 | Trade Paperback | Fiction | 416 pp | $14.99 | ISBN 9781401341701
Voice | hyperionbooks.com | margaretleroy.com
Also available as: eBook

CONVERSATION STARTERS

1. Discuss the ways in which *The Soldier's Wife* is like a fairy tale, as well as the important ways in which it is not. Discuss the running motif of fairy tales throughout the book. Is Leroy using the fairy tales as symbols, or metaphors, or as a way of constructing a thematic statement for the book? (Or, perhaps, all three?)

2. Consider the ways the setting of *The Soldier's Wife* is used as a literary device. Discuss scenes where the landscape foreshadows events or parallels the moods of the characters (in particular, Vivienne).

3. How effectively do you think Leroy portrayed life on the island of Guernsey during its occupation by the Germans in World War II? In particular, discuss the extent to which she depicted the bombing of the harbor, the decline into poverty and resourcefulness of the island's inhabitants, and the relationships between the German soldiers and the British citizens.

4. Similarly, consider—by way of the book's characters—how the different generations were affected by the war? In what ways did each generation suffer because of the war, and in what ways were they changed?

5. Comment on Vivienne's honest appraisal of her marriage early in the novel, before her relationship with Gunther begins. What does it say about her that she never confronted Eugene about his mistress?

6. Some of the less developed characters in the novel are interesting nonetheless. Discuss the roles Gwen, Angie, Max, and Johnnie play in the book and in Vivienne's life. How does each character teach her something?

7. Discuss Kirill and his role in the novel, too. When Millie began speaking about the "white ghost" in the barn, did you suspect she was talking about a man from the work camp? In what ways was he responsible for a change in Vivienne, particularly as a character in opposition to Gunther, a man who was also responsible for significant change in Vivienne?

8. When Vivienne broke off her relationship with Gunther, what did you believe? Did you believe that Gunther had reported Vivienne for housing Kirill? What did you think of Max's revelation to Vivienne that Hermann had died, and then, at the end of the book, that Gunther had not been responsible for Kirill's death?

9. In what ways is Vivienne a memorable heroine? What character trait did you find most interesting about her? What made you like her (or, possibly, dislike her) in particular?

Sophie
The Incredible True Story of the Castaway Dog
By Emma Pearse

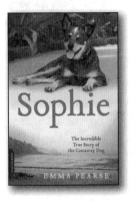

Merle's Door meets the *Daily Coyote* in this extraordinary story of a dog's journey back to her family. Sophie Tucker, a three-year-old Australian blue heeler, goes overboard into the predator infested waters of the Great Barrier Reef, and Sophie's heartbroken family has given her up for lost; little do they know that Sophie swam six miles to an isolated nature preserve called St. Bees—where she survived unassisted for five months by living off the land. The story of her survival and rescue is nothing short of miraculous.

Journalist Emma Pearse delves into Sophie's story and re-creates the accident and Sophie's improbable journey. Pearse tells the story from the perspectives of Sophie, her family, and the scientists on St. Bees who found her. Interwoven with research on the emotional lives of animals and interviews with animal experts, including Temple Grandin, Sophie offers undeniable proof about the unbreakable animal-human bond.

Heartwarming, riveting, and inspirational, Sophie is an unbelievable story of the resilience of the human—and animal—spirit.

ABOUT THE AUTHOR: **Emma Pearse** is an Australian journalist who has written for numerous publications including *New York* magazine, the *Village Voice*, the *Financial Times*, *Slate.com*, and *Salon.com*. She lives in New York City.

January 2012 | Hardcover | Nonfiction | 272 pp | $25.00 | ISBN 9780738214672
Da Capo Lifelong Books | perseusbooksgroup.com

CONVERSATION STARTERS

1. Dave and Jan believed "that childhood and family life were better with dogs." Would you agree, and why?

2. Did any of Sophie's personality traits or habits remind you of dogs you have owned? Like what?

3. What effect did Sophie have on Dave and Jan once they became empty-nesters? Can you relate to their experience in your own life? How so?

4. Do you think Dave and Jan let their feelings get in the way of their judgment in bringing Sophie on the boat?

5. What do you think of Dave and Jan's decision not to alert the authorities about Sophie's disappearance? What would you have done if you were in their situation?

6. Did Dave and Jan's reaction to Sophie's disappearance surprise you considering they had said that "they had always loved their dogs, but they were not sentimental"?

7. Did you think it was a good idea so soon after Sophie's disappearance to give Dave and Jan a new puppy? How did the new puppy, Ruby, impact the Griffith family, and how did she differ from Sophie in their eyes? And do you think it made it easier or harder for them to cope with the loss of Sophie?

8. Why do you think Sophie was able to survive in the open ocean and for five months on the islands of Keswick and St. Bees? Is it explained, as Australian vet Rob McMahon says, by the fact that it "would take a dog as tough as a cattle dog to do it," or could there be some other explanation?

9. Was Jan's sense of Sophie's being alive when Dave and she were on St. Bees just wishful thinking, or was it a premonition?

10. Why do you think Sophie chose not to respond when several people who lived on the island, including Peter Berck, offered her food and companionship? Do you think it was out of loyalty to the Griffith family, as suggested in the book?

11. How did Sophie's extraordinary return home affect the relationships between members of the Griffith family—Dave, Jan, Bridget, Luke, and Ellen?

12. Have you ever experienced or heard of a similar story of a dog or other pet overcoming tremendous adversity?

13. What does this story say about the bond between pets and their owners?

The Sublime Engine
A Biography of the Human Heart
By Stephen Amidon and Thomas Amidon, MD

A narrative history of our most essential organ, drawing on science, religion, and literature to tell the story of humankind's enduring fascination with the heart. The heart has always captured the human imagination. It is the repository of our deepest religious and artistic impulses, the organ whose steady functioning is understood, both literally and symbolically, as the very life force itself. *The Sublime Engine* explores the profound sense of awe every person feels when they ponder the miracle encased within the ribs.

In this lyrical history, a critically acclaimed novelist and a leading cardiologist—who happen to be brothers—draw upon history, science, religion, popular culture, and literature to illuminate all of the heart's physical and figurative chambers. Divided into six sections, *The Sublime Engine* traces the heart's sway over the human imagination from the time of the Egyptians and ancient Greece, through the Middle Ages and Renaissance, up to the modern era and beyond. More than just a work of scientific or cultural history, it is a biography of the single most important symbol of our humanity.

"*The Sublime Engine* *is that rare book; so entertaining that its ability to educate seems effortless.*" —**Publishers Weekly, starred review**

"*Lyrically written . . . fascinating and engaging . . . should appeal to both poets and physicians.*" —**Booklist**

ABOUT THE AUTHORS: **Stephen Amidon** is the author of six novels, including *The New City* and *Human Capital*. His fiction has been published in 15 countries, and he is a regular contributor of essays and criticism to newspapers and magazines in the United States and United Kingdom. **Thomas Amidon, MD,** has been cardiology section chief at Overlake Hospital in Bellevue, Washington, and a clinical instructor at Washington University. He is the author of dozens of articles and coauthor of the cardiology chapter in a top selling medical textbook.

January 2011 | Hardcover | Nonfiction | 256 pp | $24.95 | ISBN 9781605295848
Rodale Books | rodale.com | stephenamidon.com
Also available as: eBook and Audiobook

CONVERSATION STARTERS

1. The progression of the heart's narrative in the book focuses largely on the discovery of medical and scientific facts about the cardiac muscle. The authors, however, return time and time again to the heart as a metaphor for our most human qualities. Which interpretation of the heart resonates most with you—the empirical or the emotional? Which do you think the authors are ultimately driving at?

2. In "Ancient Heart," the authors touch on the "heart-versus-head debate," which they claim rages on to this day. How has this dispute changed over time, and how has it stayed the same—particularly as it has moved from physical to metaphorical in nature? How does the concept of right brain and left brain relate to this?

3. In "Sacred Heart," the physical heart is deemed "the one indispensable corporeal item . . . [able to] stand in for the whole man." Why do you think this was? Do you think that this idea holds true today in any sense?

4. *Frankenstein* is described as "a portrait of the heart's endurance as a metaphor even as technology mystifies the body." The authors point out that scientific exploration of the heart's anatomical and physiological properties only drove artists and theologians to cement the heart's metaphorical identity, ensuring the continuation of the human heart's central paradox. What do you think drove artists, authors, poets, and theologians to stake a metaphorical claim on the heart just as it seemed science might truly explain it?

5. Consider this quote from "Morbid Heart:" "Poe was very much aware of that the heart was no longer seen as solely the wellspring of love and life. It was also an agent of terrors that could be uncanny, even unspeakable." How does Poe's view of the heart compare to Plato's theories on the division of the soul? How does each relate to its respective era's knowledge of cardiology?

6. How do you think the book's central theme of the heart being dichotomously metaphorical and empirical relates to the careers of the two authors?

7. What do you think the future holds for the human heart? Will its journey towards immortality be thwarted by human weakness as the authors suggest? Will all of the things it represents render the heart eternal or ephemeral?

The Summer of Us

By Holly Chamberlin

The little beach house has a rickety porch and no closets, but the location is unbeatable—close to a gorgeous shoreline and the best nightlife on Martha's Vineyard. All in all, more than enough to entice three total strangers into a house share for the summer.

At first, the only thing Gincy, Danielle, and Clare have in common is a desire to spend weekends away from the city. No-nonsense Gincy has worked hard to leave her small-town childhood behind. Danielle grew up with every advantage and is looking for a husband who'll fit neatly into her pampered life, while Clare is enjoying a last burst of independence before marrying her ambitious fiancé. Yet lazy beach days and warm, conversation-filled nights forge an unexpected connection. And over the course of one eventful summer, Gincy, Danielle, and Clare will discover that friendship isn't always measured in how well you know a person's past—but in opening each other's eyes to everything the future could hold.

"The Summer of Us *is a great choice for your summertime beach reads. A clever mix of sassy attitude and romance, I found myself eagerly turning pages to find out what happened next.*"—**RoundTableReviews.com**

ABOUT THE AUTHOR: **Holly Chamberlin** is a native New Yorker, but she now lives in Boston—the aftermath of stumbling across Mr. Right at the one moment she wasn't watching the terrain. She's been writing and editing—poetry, children's fantasies, a romance novel or two, among many other genres and projects—her entire life. She has two cats, Jack and Betty, and when she's not writing her hobbies include reading, shopping and cocktails at six.

April 2011 | Trade Paperback | Fiction | 432 pp | $9.95 | ISBN 9780758265739
Kensington Books | kensingtonbooks.com | hollychamberlin.com
Also available as: eBook

CONVERSATION STARTERS

1. In the beginning of the book, Gincy presents herself as "the go-to girl." Clare says that she's "pleasant and easy to please." Danielle claims to have good self-esteem. By the end of the book, how might each character's self description have changed?

2. How might the brother-sister relationships have influenced each character's chosen lifestyle or romantic decisions? The father-daughter relationships? The mother-daughter relationships?

3. Discuss the notion of privacy in a committed relationship. Consider Clare and her concerns about keeping a secret journal.

4. Explore how each character views marriage. In what ways are their views naïve or mature?

5. Discuss the notion of a "leap of faith"—what is required when we've told ourselves we want one thing and quite another thing suddenly presents itself as a viable option. How does each character take—or not take—that leap?

6. At one point Rick says, "Life is short, Gincy. When something good happens, you embrace it." But it's not always easy to determine what is good for us at any given moment. Discuss this in relation to Gincy, Clare, and Danielle.

7. Discuss the notion of honesty and fidelity, lying versus not telling the entire truth, in the case of each character.

8. Clare tells us that she is no longer in love with Win, but that she does still love him "in the way you love someone you know so well it's almost like loving yourself. Or, at least, being used to yourself." Discuss the validity of love as habit, or its lack thereof.

9. Win's brother Trey says, "Family owes something to family. Even if it's just pretending to get along." Do you agree?

10. At one point Clare says, "You can get over anger . . . Hurt, too, can be mended . . . But sadness is different. It doesn't seem to ever go away; it rests deep inside. Sadness is profound disappointment." Discuss this.

11. Clare wonders if longevity in a marriage is a worthwhile accomplishment if the years together are "bland, possibly soulless." She also assumes that in a long-term exclusive relationship it is impossible to experience "flashes of supreme passion and knowledge." Do you agree?

12. Rick believes that "Life can't be about expectation. . . . Nothing's ever as you expect it to be. Life has to be about risk. If you want to be happy, there's no other way." Discuss this in relation to Gincy, Clare, and Danielle.

The Surrendered

By Chang-rae Lee

The bestselling and award-winning author of *Native Speaker*, *A Gesture Life*, and *Aloft* returns with his most ambitious novel yet—a spellbinding story of how love and war echo through an entire lifetime.

June Han was orphaned as a girl by the Korean War. Hector Brennan was a young GI who fled the petty tragedies of his small town to serve his country. When the war ended, their lives collided at a Korean orphanage, where they vied for the attention of Sylvie Tanner, a beautiful yet deeply damaged missionary.

As Lee masterfully unfurls the stunning story of June, Hector, and Sylvie, he weaves a profound meditation on the nature of heroism and sacrifice, the power of love, and the possibilities for mercy, salvation, and surrendering oneself to another.

"This is not a happy book, but it is a rewarding one. The Surrendered grabs your attention—sometimes terrifying you in the process—and doesn't let go until its final moment. . . . Its pages are breathtakingly alive." —**The San Francisco Chronicle**

"[Chang-rae Lee's] largest, most ambitious book." —**The New York Times Book Review**

About the Author: **Chang-rae Lee** is the author of *Native Speaker*, winner of the Hemingway Foundation/PEN Award for first fiction, *A Gesture Life*, and *Aloft*. Selected by *The New Yorker* as one of the twenty best writers under forty, Chang-rae Lee teaches writing at Princeton University.

March 2011 | Trade Paperback | Fiction | 496 pp | $16.00 | ISBN 9781594485015
Riverhead Books | penguin.com
Also available as: eBook and Audiobook

CONVERSATION STARTERS

1. In the orphanage, June is a bully to the other children and shows affection only to Sylvie. Yet when we first meet her, she is incredibly caring to her sister and brother. What do you think caused this change in her personality? How did her experiences as a young girl shape the adult she became?

2. Hector seems to develop true feelings for Dora. If things had ended differently in the final scene with Dora, do you think he would still have gone off with June? Why or why not? Do you think his experience with Sylvie colored his relationship with Dora? How?

3. Do you think Sylvie would have adopted June had things not happened the way they did? Why or why not?

4. June seems fixated on finding Nicholas even after it becomes clear that he is not who he says he is. Why do you think she is so focused? Why do you think she needs to find him?

5. If you've read Chang-rae Lee's work in the past, you know that he writes often of identity. How do these themes play out in *The Surrendered*? Of Hector, June, and Sylvie, which character do you think has the strongest sense of identity? The weakest?

6. Each character undergoes a traumatic experience that ends up shaping the course of his or her life: Hector's father's death, June's loss of her family, and Sylvie's experience in Manchuria. How do these events change their characters? Do you think each person's life would be different had these traumatic events not occurred?

7. The book *A Memory of Solferino* appears throughout the novel and is passed from Sylvie to June to Nicholas. What do you think the book means to each character and how does it influence the choices they make?

8. Although *The Surrendered* is very much about war, the events of the Korean War itself make up a very small part of the book. Why do you think the author chose this approach? What point do you think he was making? How does this relate to his choice of title?

9. Discuss the idea of mercy in the book. Which characters do you think most exemplify this trait? In which scenes does the idea of mercy seem to be the guiding force?

10. Hector is born in the town of Ilion and is named after Hector in the *Iliad*. Discuss heroism in the book. Are any of the characters heroes? Do they behave heroically?

Swamplandia!

By Karen Russell

The Bigtree alligator-wrestling dynasty is in decline, and Swamplandia!, their island home and gator-wrestling theme park, formerly #1 in the region, is swiftly being encroached on by a fearsome and sophisticated competitor called the World of Darkness. Ava's mother, the park's indomitable headliner, has just died; her sister, Ossie, has fallen in love with a spooky character known as the Dredgeman, who may or may not be an actual ghost; and her brilliant big brother, Kiwi, who dreams of becoming a scholar, has just defected to the World of Darkness in a last-ditch effort to keep their family business from going under. Ava's father, affectionately known as Chief Bigtree, is AWOL, and that leaves Ava, a resourceful but terrified thirteen-year-old, to manage ninety-eight gators and the vast, inscrutable landscape of her own grief.

Against a backdrop of hauntingly fecund plant life animated by ancient lizards and lawless hungers, Karen Russell has written an utterly singular novel about a family's struggle to stay afloat in a world that is inexorably sinking. An arrestingly beautiful and inventive work from a vibrant new voice in fiction.

"Vividly worded, exuberant in characterization, the novel is a wild ride. . . . This family, wrestling with their desires and demons . . . will lodge in the memories of anyone lucky enough to read Swamplandia!*"* —**The New York Times Book Review**

ABOUT THE AUTHOR: **Karen Russell**, a native of Miami, has been featured in *The New Yorker*'s debut fiction issue and on *The New Yorker*'s 20 Under 40 list, and was chosen as one of *Granta*'s Best Young American Novelists. In 2009, she received the 5 Under 35 award from the National Book Foundation. Three of her short stories have been selected for the *Best American Short Stories* volumes. She is currently writer-in-residence at Bard College.

July 2011 | Trade Paperback | Fiction | 416 pp | $14.95 | ISBN 9780307276681
Vintage | readinggroupcenter.com
Also available as: eBook and Audiobook

CONVERSATION STARTERS

1. Now that you've read the novel, go back and reread the epigraph. Why do you think Russell chose this quote?

2. Some of these characters first appeared in the story "Ava Wrestles the Alligator" in Russell's collection, *St. Lucy's Home for Girls Raised by Wolves*. Have you read that story? How does it compare to the novel?

3. How did Chief's myth-making affect his children? How might things have been different if he'd been more truthful?

4. Where else does the notion of evolution come into play?

5. Why do you think Ossie sees Louis and other ghosts, but never Hilola?

6. What does Ava's red alligator represent? And the melaleuca trees?

7. Why do you think Russell interrupted the novel for the story of the Dredgeman's Revelation? What exactly is the "revelation"?

8. There are biblical references throughout the book, especially in the World of Darkness sections. Why does Russell include them?

9. How do Kiwi's actions affect his family? What do we learn via his sojourn on the mainland?

10. The three Bigtree children are innocent for their ages. Which one matures the most over the course of the novel?

11. The Bird Man calls the ending of the Dredgeman's Revelation "a vanishing point." (page 221) What does he mean by that?

12. Both the Bird Man and Vijay act as guides to a Bigtree sibling. How does each approach his role?

13. When Ava said "I love you" to the Bird Man on page 245, what did you expect to happen as a result?

14. Did the Bird Man believe in the underworld, or did he have an ulterior motive all along?

15. How does Kiwi's use of language change during the novel? What does it reflect?

16. Like the Dredgeman, several of the Bigtrees have revelations. Whose is the most surprising?

This Glittering World
By T. Greenwood

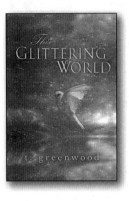

One November morning, Ben Bailey walks out of his Flagstaff, Arizona, home to retrieve the paper. Instead, he finds Ricky Begay, a young Navajo man, beaten and dying in the newly fallen snow.

Unable to forget the incident, especially once he meets Ricky's sister, Shadi, Ben begins to question everything, from his job as a part-time history professor to his fiancée, Sara. When Ben first met Sara, he was mesmerized by her optimism and easy confidence. These days, their relationship only reinforces a loneliness that stretches back to his fractured childhood.

Ben decides to discover the truth about Ricky's death, both for Shadi's sake and in hopes of filling in the cracks in his own life. Yet the answers leave him torn—between responsibility and happiness, between his once-certain future and the choices that could liberate him from a delicate web of lies he has spun.

"Stark, taut, and superbly written, this dark tale brims with glimpses of the Southwest and scenes of violence, gruesome but not gratuitous. This haunting look at a fractured family is certain to please readers of literary suspense."
—**Library Journal** (**starred review**)

ABOUT THE AUTHOR: **T. Greenwood** is the author of 5 novels, including *Two Rivers,* an IndieBound selection, *Breathing Water, Nearer Than the Sky,* and *Undressing the Moon,* the latter two both Booksense 76 picks. She has received grants from the Sherwood Anderson Foundation, the Christopher Isherwood Foundation and, most recently, the National Endowment for the Arts. Greenwood currently resides in San Diego, California, with family, where she teaches creative writing at UCSD's Extension Program and for San Diego Writers, Ink at The Ink Spot.

January 2011 | Trade Paperback | Fiction | 288 pp | $15.00 | ISBN 9780758250919
Kensington Books | kensingtonbooks.com | tgreenwood.com
Also available as: eBook

CONVERSATION STARTERS

1. Discuss Ben's relationship with Sara and how it changes through the course of the novel. Why is he attracted to Shadi? What does she represent to Ben?

2. Ben experienced two significant losses as a young boy (the death of his sister and his father's abandonment). How did these two traumas shape him as a man?

3. How does Ben's relationship with his own father affect his decision to stay with Sara when she discovers that she is pregnant? Do you think he would have made a good father?

4. Why do you think Ben became so involved with finding out what happened to Ricky? Was it a sense of morality? A sense of responsibility? Or was it really for Shadi? Do you think Ben would have done everything he did if he weren't attracted to Shadi?

5. If you were in a similar situation to Ben's, if you had woken up, gone out to get the newspaper, and found someone near death in the snow, what would you have done? Would you have dropped the whole thing and let the police ignore an obvious case of assault?

6. There is a great deal of injustice in this novel: from the original crime committed against Ricky to the police department's initial dismissal of his death as an alcohol related accident. At one point in the novel, Lucky suggests that there is "no such thing" as justice. Do you agree? If not, is justice served at the end of the novel? And, if so, at what expense?

7. At one point, Shadi calls Ben selfish. Do you agree with her? What does he do that's selfish, and what does he do that's selfless?

8. How much do you think Sara really knew about what was going on? Do you think she knew Shadi was related to Ricky when she told Ben she wanted the rug commissioned? Do you think she knew Ben was involved with Shadi?

9. Near the end of the novel, Shadi gives Ben an ultimatum, demanding that he choose between her and Sara. Is this, ultimately, truly his choice? Do you believe he will keep his promise and stay with Sara?

10. The definition of a tragedy is a story in which the hero comes to ruin or experiences tremendous sorrow as the result of both circumstance and a disastrous character flaw. In tragedies, readers should experience both fear and pity for the hero. Would you call Ben a tragic hero and this novel a tragedy? What is Ben's tragic flaw?

Threading the Needle

By Marie Bostwick

The economic downturn has hit New Bern, Connecticut, and Tessa Woodruff's herbal apothecary shop, For the Love of Lavender, is suffering. So is her once-happy thirty-four-year marriage to Lee. They'd given up everything to come back to New Bern from Boston and start their business, but now they're wondering if they made the right decision. To relieve the strain, Tessa signs up for a quilting class at the Cobbled Court Quilt Shop, and to her surprise, rediscovers the power of sisterhood—along with the childhood friend she thought she'd lost forever. Madelyn Beecher left New Bern twenty years ago and never looked back. But when her husband is convicted of running a Ponzi scheme and she's left with nothing but her late grandmother's cottage, she is forced to return to the town she fled. Unfortunately, the cottage is in terrible shape.

Madelyn's only hope is to transform it into an inn. But to succeed, she'll need the help of her fellow quilters, including the one friend she never thought she'd see again—or forgive. Now Madelyn and Tessa will have to relive old memories, forge new ones, and realize it's possible to start over, one stitch at a time—as long as you're surrounded by friends.

"[A] buoyant novel about the value of friendship . . . a tantalizing book club contender."—**Publishers Weekly**

About the Author: **Marie Bostwick** was born and raised in the Northwest. Since marrying the love of her life twenty-four years ago, she has never known a moment's boredom. Marie and her family have moved a score of times, living in eight U.S. states and two Mexican cities, and collecting a vast and cherished array of friends and experiences. Marie has three handsome sons and now lives with her husband in Connecticut where she writes, reads, quilts, and is active in her local church.

May 2011 | Trade Paperback | Fiction | 352 pp | $15.00 | ISBN 9780758232175
Kensington Books | kensingtonbooks.com | mariebostwick.com
Also available as: eBook

CONVERSATION STARTERS

1. Madelyn Beecher Baron's upbringing impacted her later life decisions. How have your upbringing and your family affected your decisions? What messages or beliefs have you had to overcome? What values or beliefs from your childhood have worked well for you?

2. Madelyn and Tessa both return to New Bern after being gone for many years. Madelyn returned resentfully because she had nowhere else to go and no other way to live. Tessa moved back to fulfill a dream. Have you ever left a place or situation that you later returned to for one reason or another? How did the return work out for you?

3. Financial struggle and fulfilling a dream play key roles in *Threading the Needle*. How has financial struggle led you in a direction you might not otherwise have considered, like Madelyn? Describe a time you had to defer or give up a dream, like Tessa, because of finances. How did this change in direction work out for you?

4. Jake Kaminski, rumored to be a ladies' man, shares his story of recovery from alcoholism with Madelyn, and he offers her unconditional support. Why does he do this? How does this help Madelyn?

5. Many of the characters in the Cobbled Court series own a business. If you could start your own business, what kind of business would that be? What do you think are the benefits and challenges of working for yourself? Do you think your personality is suited for being a business owner? Why or why not?

6. When Tessa was younger, her mother advised her to "Enjoy the little things in life, Tessa. One day you may look back and realize they were the big things." Do you think that is true? If so, what little things in your life have you realized are truly the big things?

7. Madelyn realizes after opening her bed-and-breakfast, which so many New Bern residents supported, that, "This is what it's like to be part of something, of some place. This is what it's like to care." What have you been part of that's been meaningful to you?

8. Madelyn finds her childhood quilt in the Beecher Cottage attic. Tessa pays to have it repaired, and then the quilt ends up on one of the beds in Madelyn's bed-and-breakfast. Discuss the symbolism of quilting in the story and to its characters. Near the end of the book, the quilters decide to make a baby quilt for Angela, who was also betrayed by a man. What's the significance of this scene?

The Tiger's Wife
By Téa Obreht

WINNER OF THE ORANGE PRIZE FOR FICTION

In a Balkan country mending from war, Natalia, a young doctor, is compelled to unravel the mysterious circumstances surrounding her beloved grandfather's recent death. Searching for clues, she turns to his worn copy of *The Jungle Book* and the stories he told her of his encounters over the years with "the deathless man." But most extraordinary of all is the story her grandfather never told her—the legend of the tiger's wife.

"*Stunning . . . a hugely ambitious, audaciously written work. . . . A richly textured and searing novel.*" —**Michiko Kakutani, The New York Times**

"*Written in a wry, classical, luxuriant style reminiscent of Tolstoy. . . .* [The Tiger's Wife] *would be a spectacular accomplishment under any circumstance, but the fact that Obreht is only 25 years old makes the whole thing downright supernatural.*" —*Marie Claire*

"*Téa Obreht is the most thrilling literary discovery in years.*" —**Colum McCann, author of Let the Great World Spin**

ABOUT THE AUTHOR: **Téa Obreht** was born in Belgrade in the former Yugoslavia in 1985 and has lived in the United States since the age of twelve. Her writing has appeared in *The New Yorker* and *The Atlantic*, and is forthcoming in *The Best American Short Stories* and *The Best American Nonrequired Reading*. She lives in Ithaca, New York.

November 2011 | Trade Paperback | Fiction | 368 pp | $15.00 | ISBN 9780385343848
Random House Trade Paperbacks | randomhouse.com | teaobreht.com

CONVERSATION STARTERS

1. Natalia says that the key to her grandfather's life and death "lies between two stories: the story of the tiger's wife, and the story of the deathless man". What power do the stories we tell about ourselves have to shape our identity and help us understand our lives?

2. Which of the different ways the characters go about making peace with the dead felt familiar from your own life? Which took you by surprise?

3. Natalia believes that her grandfather's memories of the village apothecary "must have been imperishable." What lesson do you think he might have learned from what happened to the apothecary?

4. What significance does the tiger have to the different characters in the novel: Natalia, her grandfather, the tiger's wife, the villagers? Why do you think Natalia's grandfather's reaction to the tiger's appearance in the village was so different than the rest of the villagers?

5. "The story of this war—dates, names, who started it, why—that belongs to everyone," Natalia's grandfather tells her. But "those moments you keep to yourself" are more important. By eliding place names and specific events of recent Balkan history, what do you think the author is doing?

6. When the deathless man and the grandfather share a last meal before the bombing of Sarobor, the grandfather urges the deathless man to tell the waiter his fate so he can go home and be with his family. Is Gavran Gailé right to decide to stop telling people that they are going to die? Would you rather know your death was coming or go "in suddenness"?

7. Did knowing more about Luka's past make him more sympathetic? Why do you think the author might have chosen to give the backstories of Luka, Dariša the Bear, and the apothecary?

8. The copy of *The Jungle Book* Natalia's grandfather always carries around in his coat pocket is not among the possessions she collects after his death. What do you think happens to it?

9. The novel moves back and forth between myth and modern-day "real life." What did you think of the juxtaposition of folklore and contemporary realism?

10. Of all the themes of this novel (war, storytelling, family, death, myth, etc.) which one resonated the most for you?

Tiny Sunbirds, Far Away

By Christie Watson

When their mother catches their father with another woman, twelve year-old Blessing and her fourteen-year-old brother, Ezikiel, are forced to leave their comfortable home in Lagos for the village in the Niger Delta, to live with their mother's family. Without running water or electricity, Warri is at first a nightmare for Blessing. Her mother is gone all day and works suspiciously late into the night to pay the children's school fees. Her brother, once a promising student, seems to be falling increasingly under the influence of the local group of violent teenage boys calling themselves Freedom Fighters. Her grandfather, a kind if misguided man, is trying on Islam as his new religion of choice, and is even considering the possibility of bringing in a second wife.

But Blessing's grandmother, wise and practical, soon becomes a beloved mentor, teaching Blessing the ways of the midwife in rural Nigeria. Blessing is exposed to the horrors of genital mutilation and the devastation wrought on the environment by British and American oil companies. As Warri comes to feel like home, Blessing becomes increasingly aware of the threats to its safety, both from its unshakable but dangerous traditions and the relentless carelessness of the modern world.

"Tiny Sunbirds, Far Away *is the witty and beautifully written story of one family's attempt to survive a new life they could never have imagined."*
—*GoodReads*

ABOUT THE AUTHOR: **Christie Watson** trained as a pediatric nurse at Great Ormond Street Hospital in London and worked as a senior staff nurse and educator for over ten years before joining the University of East Anglia for her MA in Creative Writing. There she won the Malcolm Bradbury Bursary for her work. Watson lives in South London with her Nigerian Muslim partner and their large dual-heritage family.

May 2011 | Trade Paperback | Fiction | 448 pp | $15.95 | ISBN 9781590514665
Other Press | otherpress.com | christiewatson.com
Also available as: eBook and Audiobook

CONVERSATION STARTERS

1. Ezikiel and Blessing share a special sibling bond. How did it change when they moved from Lagos to Warri? Do you think there was anything that Blessing could have done to save Ezikiel?

2. Blessing tells her story in her own distinct voice. How would you characterize her style as a narrator? Discuss Blessing's development from an unsure, shy girl to a confident young woman. How does each character in the novel encourage—or stifle—Blessing's maturation?

3. Watson originally tried writing *Tiny Sunbirds, Far Away* from the perspective of Dan, the white oil worker. How would Dan's perspective have changed the book? What insights might his narration have brought to the novel? What limitations might Watson have faced?

4. From the very first line of the novel, "Father was a loud man," it's clear that her father is of crucial importance to Blessing. How does her opinion of him change throughout the story? How does her relationship with him affect her relationships with the other men in her life?

5. Discuss the power of the women in *Tiny Sunbirds, Far Away* (Grandma's rally) versus the power of men in the novel (Alhaji, the Sibeye Boys). How does the expression of power differ between the genders?

6. It's estimated that three million girls are at risk of female genital mutilation in Africa. Discuss Grandma's choice to perform the practice. How does it inform Blessing's own career as a midwife? How do Grandma and Blessing determine where to draw the line between ethical responsibility and cultural tradition?

7. Legend and tradition play significant roles in Blessing's family—from Grandma's stories to Alhaji's disbelief in Ezikiel's medical condition. How are religion, education, and tradition balanced in the novel? Do they coexist? When and why do they clash?

8. Though foreign companies and Nigeria's own government gain enormous wealth from the oil industry, the majority of people residing in the oil producing regions of the country continue to live in extreme poverty. How does the presence of the oil industry impact the lives of the characters in the novel? Does Watson offer any hints as to what could be done to better the situation?

To the End of the Land
By David Grossman

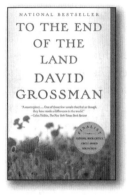

Ora, a middle-aged Israeli mother, is on the verge of celebrating her son Ofer's release from army service when he returns to the front for a major offensive. In a fit of preemptive grief and magical thinking, she sets out for a hike in the Galilee, leaving no forwarding information for the "notifiers" who might darken her door with the worst possible news. Recently estranged from her husband, Ilan, she drags along an unlikely companion: their former best friend and her former lover Avram, once a brilliant artistic spirit. Avram served in the army alongside Ilan when they were young, but their lives were forever changed one weekend when the two jokingly had Ora draw lots to see which of them would get the few days' leave being offered by their commander—a chance act that sent Avram into Egypt and the Yom Kippur War, where he was brutally tortured as POW. In the aftermath, he refused to keep in touch with the family and has never met the boy. Now, as Ora and Avram sleep out in the hills, ford rivers, and cross valleys, avoiding all news from the front, she gives him the gift of Ofer, word by word; she supplies the whole story of her motherhood, a retelling that keeps Ofer very much alive for Ora and for the reader, and opens Avram to human bonds undreamed of in his broken world. Their walk has a "war and peace" rhythm, as their conversation places the most hideous trials of war next to the joys and anguish of raising children. Never have we seen so clearly the reality and surreality of daily life in Israel, the currents of ambivalence about war within one household, and the burdens that fall on each generation anew.

*"A masterpiece. . . . One of the few novels that feel as though they have made a difference to the world." —***The New York Times Book Review**

ABOUT THE AUTHOR: **David Grossman** was born in Jerusalem. He is the author of numerous works of fiction, nonfiction, and children's literature. His work has appeared in *The New Yorker* and has been translated into thirty languages around the world.

August 2011 | Trade Paperback | Fiction | 672 pp | $15.95 | ISBN 9780307476401
Vintage | readinggroupcenter.com
Also available as: eBook and Audiobook

CONVERSATION STARTERS

TO THE END
OF THE
LAND
DAVID
GROSSMAN

1. What one word would you use to describe the central theme of this novel? Is it a political novel?

2. In an interview, Grossman said about grief, "The first feeling you have is one of exile. You are being exiled from everything you know." How do both grief and exile figure into this story?

3. Throughout the novel is the notion of tapestry, of threads being woven. What does that tapestry signify?

4. Ora says, "I'm no good at saving people." Why does she say this? Is it true?

5. What function does Sami serve in the novel? What do we learn about Ora through her interactions with him?

6. Why does Ora consider Ofer's reenlistment to be a betrayal? Why do his whispered, on-camera instructions affect her so strongly?

7. Discuss Adam's assertion that Ora is "an unnatural mother." What do you think he means by that? What does Ora take it to mean?

8. What is the significance of Ofer's film, in which there are no physical beings, only their shadows?

9. In both Adam and Ofer, the influence of nature vs. nurture seems quite fluid. How is each like his biological father, and how does each resemble the man to whom he is not related by blood?

10. What role does food play in the novel? What does vegetarianism, especially, signify?

11. Why does Ora refuse to go back for her notebook? As a reader, could you identify with Ora's actions? What about elsewhere in the novel?

12. What do we learn about Ora, Ilan, and Ofer through the story of Adam's compulsive behavior? What is "the force of *no*"?

13. Discuss the significance of whose name Ora draws from the hat. Did she choose that person intentionally? How might the lives of Ora, Ilan, and Avram have been different if the other name were drawn?

14. When Ora says to Avram, "Maybe you'll even have a girl," what is she really saying?

15. Discuss the final scene of the novel. What does Avram's vision signify? Was Ora's motivation for the hike wrong, as she fears?

16. How did Grossman's personal note at the end change your experience of the novel? What seems possible for Ora and Avram, and the other characters in the book, at the end of the story?

The True Memoirs of Little K

By Adrienne Sharp

Exiled in Paris, tiny, one-hundred-year-old Mathilde Kschessinska sits down to write her memoirs before all that she believes to be true is forgotten. A lifetime ago, she was the vain, ambitious, impossibly charming *prima ballerina assoluta* of the tsar's Russian Imperial Ballet in St. Petersburg. Now, as she looks back on her tumultuous life, she can still recall every slight she ever suffered, every conquest she ever made.

Before the revolution, Kschessinska dominated that world as the greatest dancer of her age. At seventeen, her crisp technique made her a star. So did her romance with the tsarevich Nicholas Romanov, soon to be Nicholas II. It was customary for grand dukes and sons of tsars to draw their mistresses from the ranks of the ballet, but it was not customary for them to fall in love.

When Nicholas ascended to the throne as tsar, he was forced to give up his mistress, and Kschessinska turned for consolation to his cousins, two grand dukes with whom she formed an ménage à trois. But when Nicholas's marriage to Alexandra wavered after she produced girl after girl, he came once again to visit his Little K. As the tsar's empire began its fatal crumble, Kschessinka's devotion to the imperial family would be tested in ways she could never have foreseen.

"Sharp's knowledge of ballet and her lush, descriptive writing give depth and resonance to this imagined history." —Kirkus

About the Author: **Adrienne Sharp** entered the world of ballet at age seven and trained at the prestigious Harkness Ballet in New York. She received her M.A. with honors from the Writing Seminars at the Johns Hopkins University. She is the author of *White Swan, Black Swan* and *The Sleeping Beauty*.

October 2011 | Trade Paperback | Fiction | 384 pp | $15.00 | ISBN 978-0312610715
Picador | PicadorUSA.com | adriennesharp.com
Also available as: eBook

CONVERSATION STARTERS

1. The novel's title claims these are Mathilde's true memoirs. Is any memoir entirely true? What aspects of his or her life might a memoirist attempt to conceal—or rewrite? What is illuminating about reading a fictionalized account of someone's life as opposed to an autobiography or a biography?

2. In what ways did Mathilde's affair with Nicholas give her both more power and less? Consider her position both in the theater and in society.

3. The love between Nicholas and Mathilde was affected from the start by the knowledge that they could never be husband and wife. How did this knowledge define their relationship early on, and how did their expectations of each other change over time as their relationship continued?

4. Discuss Rasputin's role in the Romanov family. Why did Alix obstinately ignore the furor that surrounded Rasputin, a furor that became one of the incendiary factors in the people's anger against their sovereigns? In what ways did Rasputin's murder foreshadow the revolution and the strike at the crown two months later?

5. What advantage does Mathilde have over Nicholas, imprisoned at Tsarskoye Selo, when she makes her decision to retrieve her son before the family is moved to Siberia? What future does Nicholas envision for himself and his family at that point, the summer of 1917—and what future does Mathilde see ahead for them?

6. Which of Mathilde's history lessons surprised you the most? What aspects of the Russian revolution had you been unaware of? Was a violent revolution, resulting in a brutal police state, the only way the suffering of the lower classes could have been resolved in that society?

7. Once Mathilde and the Romanovs find themselves in exile, they attempt to re-create their former lives—but the rules that formerly governed that society have loosened, enabling Mathilde's marriage to Andrei. What did each of them gain from this marriage—and in what ways did it help to legitimize Vova's place in Russian society in exile?

8. In the novel's closing pages, Mathilde is proud that her name appears in the genealogy charts of European and Russian royalty, though she expresses disappointment that her name is not included next to Nicholas' and that her son's name does not appear at all. Does she, after all, find the sacrifices she made and her exclusion from a place in normal society and normal family life worth this status?

....

Turn of Mind

By Alice LaPlante

A stunning first novel, both literary and thriller, about a retired orthopedic surgeon with dementia, *Turn of Mind* has already received worldwide attention. Alice LaPlante brings us deep into a brilliant woman's deteriorating mind, where the impossibility of recognizing reality can be both a blessing and a curse.

As the book opens, Dr. Jennifer White's best friend, Amanda, who lived down the block, has been killed, and four fingers surgically removed from her hand. Dr. White is the prime suspect and she herself doesn't know whether she did it. Told in White's own voice, fractured and eloquent, a picture emerges of the surprisingly intimate, complex alliance between these life-long friends—two proud, forceful women who were at times each other's most formidable adversaries. As the investigation into the murder deepens and White's relationships with her live-in caretaker and two grown children intensify, a chilling question lingers: is White's shattered memory preventing her from revealing the truth or helping her to hide it?

A startling portrait of a disintegrating mind clinging to bits of reality through anger, frustration, shame, and unspeakable loss, *Turn of Mind* examines the deception and frailty of memory and how it defines our very existence.

"Turn of Mind *is a uniquely entertaining literary thriller. Alice LaPlante's portrayal of the prime suspect's escalating dementia, told from her point of view, is gripping, unnerving, and utterly brilliant."* —**Lisa Genova,** *New York Times* **bestselling author of** *Still Alice*

About the Author: **Alice LaPlante** is an award-winning writer who teaches at San Francisco State University and Stanford University, where she was awarded a Wallace Stegner Fellowship and held a Jones Lectureship. Raised in Chicago, she now lives with her family in Northern California.

July 2011 | Hardcover | Fiction | 320 pp | $24.00 | ISBN 9780802119773
Grove Atlantic | groveatlantic.com
Also available as: eBook and Audiobook

CONVERSATION STARTERS

1. What is the time span of the novel? Were you clear about the flashbacks in Jennifer's memory? Even in her surreal perceptions, is she still working out the past in the stories of James, Mark, Fiona, Amanda, and Peter? What about Dr. Tsu? Is the past really the past in *Turn of Mind*?

2. After his riding catastrophe, Christopher Reeve lay frozen in his own body. He said to his wife, "I'm still here." The essential Christopher was in there somewhere like the butterfly in the bell jar. Is that true of Jennifer? Which character do you think is able to see that essence the way Reeve's wife could?

3. What draws Jennifer and Amanda together? What locks them in a friendship/competition like a pair of magnets that often get turned around, wrong end to?

4. What surprised you about the marriage of Jennifer and James? How well do you think you know James? James, described as a creature of darkness, is known for "keeping his own counsel on things of import" (p. 47). What were these things? Why are they important in unraveling the mysteries of the book?

5. How does Jennifer refuse to be discounted? Even paranoiac, she has power. (Or is it paranoia when indeed everyone around her is set to restrain her or to humor her—patronize her, as she says.)

6. What is it about Jennifer that makes her so compelling, appealing, even? She behaves badly, outrageously, but there is a larger-than-life element in her that we admire. Give examples.

7. What is the Russian icon? How does it, as a symbol, work on multiple levels? Describe it. What is its history to Jennifer and James, Amanda, Mark, and Fiona?

8. Peter, in a prescient moment, says, "It's those damned cicadas. . . . They make one think about Old Testament–style wrath-of-God type things" (p. 46). What are the dreadful revelations that grow more apocalyptic as they have to repeated, again and again, to Jennifer?

9. Fiona recalls "Amanda at her worst, her supercilious morality on full display" (p. 303). What is the confrontation here between "the iconoclast and the devoted godmother" as Fiona has earlier described her?

10. "Some things shouldn't be scrutinized too closely. Some mysteries are only rendered, not solved" (p. 198). This is Jennifer to Mark about his father, but does it have relevance to the end of *Turn of Mind*? Are all the mysteries explained at the end? Are there things that still puzzle you?

The Uncoupling
By Meg Wolitzer

From the *New York Times* bestselling author of *The Ten-Year Nap*—a funny, provocative novel about female desire.

When the elliptical new drama teacher at Stellar Plains High School chooses *Lysistrata* as the school play—the comedy by Aristophanes in which women stop having sex with men in order to end a war—a strange spell seems to be cast over the school. Or, at least, over the women. One by one throughout the high school community, perfectly healthy, normal women and teenage girls turn away from their husbands and boyfriends in the bedroom, for reasons they don't really understand. As the women worry over their loss of passion and the men become by turns unhappy, offended, and above all, confused, both sides are forced to look at their shared history, and at their sexual selves in a new light.

"*Stunningly insightful, characteristically hilarious, Wolitzer's latest holds a mirror up to modern America, offering a shock of recognition amid the laughter.*" —**People (four stars)**

"*Wolitzer makes it work, thanks to sharp characterizations and acute observations on everything from the digital generation gap to the accommodations made in a long marriage. . . . A risky strategy pays off for a smart author whose work both amuses and hits home.*" —**Kirkus**

ABOUT THE AUTHOR: **Meg Wolitzer**'s novels include *The Ten-Year Nap*, *The Position*, and *The Wife*. She lives in New York City.

March 2012 | Trade Paperback | Fiction | 288 pp | $15.00 | ISBN 9781594485657
Riverhead Books | penguin.com | megwolitzer.com
Also available as: eBook and Audiobook

CONVERSATION STARTERS

1. Think about the women in the novel. Each of them reacts to the loss of desire in a different way. How does each woman's reaction reflect the stage of life she is in? Which woman do you think is the most changed at the end of the novel?

2. Willa and Miles both participate in an online world and communicate with each other electronically. How do you think electronic communication changes how relationships are built?

3. Dory and Robby seem to be the perfect couple at the start of the book. How does the author signal that there might be problems beneath the surface? Think about other books you've read that feature married couples who start off happily married. How are those marriages similar to Dory and Robby's? How are they different?

4. Think about the character of Fran. Do you think she's a force in the book for good? Do you think she's fully aware of the consequences of what she's doing? What price does she pay for her actions?

5. The play *Lysistrata* figures prominently in the book. What do you know about the play *Lysistrata*? How does the action of the play relate to the events of the book? Why do you think the author chose this play to be central to her novel? How does *Lysistrata* relate to the modern world?

6. Think about the spell. How is each woman affected by the spell? What is the significance of the moment each woman comes under the power of the spell?

7. While the spell affects the relationship between men and women, *The Uncoupling* also deals with the relationship between mothers and their children. How is Dory and Willa's relationship affected by the spell? What other mother and child relationships are in the book? How are those relationships changed by the end?

8. Neither Marissa nor Leanne is in a committed relationship at the start of the book. How does the spell change their view of their own sexuality? How is it different from the ways the married women are changed?

9. The spell of course is fantasy, but think about real-life parallels. Are there examples in your life where you can see a similar "spell" at work?

10. How does Wolitzer compare the effects of the spell of *Lysistrata* to the spell of falling in love—or out of love? Are there other experiences in life that make you feel as if you're falling under enchantment? The spell of a good book, for instance, or the spell of a play?

A Visit From the Goon Squad
By Jennifer Egan

Winner of the 2011 Pulitzer Prize for Fiction

Moving from San Francisco in the 1970s to a vividly imagined New York City sometime after 2020, Jennifer Egan portrays the interlacing lives of men and women whose desires and ambitions converge and collide as the passage of time, cultural change, and private experience define and redefine their identities. Bennie Salazar, a punk rocker in his teenage years, is facing middle age as a divorced and disheartened record producer. His cool, competent assistant, Sasha, keeps everything under control—except for her unconquerable compulsion to steal. Their diverse and diverting memories of the past and musings about the present set the stage for a cycle of tales about their friends, families, business associates, and lovers.

"Pitch perfect. . . . Darkly, rippingly funny. . . . Egan possesses a satirist's eye and a romance novelist's heart." —*The New York Times Book Review*

"At once intellectually stimulating and moving. . . . Like a masterful album, this one demands a replay." —*The San Francisco Chronicle*

"A new classic of American fiction." —*Time*

"Wildly ambitious. . . . A tour de force. . . . Music is both subject and metaphor as Egan explores the mutability of time, destiny, and individual accountability post-technology." —*O, The Oprah Magazine*

About the Author: **Jennifer Egan** is the author of *The Invisible Circus*, which was released as a feature film by Fine Line in 2001, *Emerald City and Other Stories, Look at Me*, which was nominated for the National Book Award in 2001, and the bestselling *The Keep*. Her new book, *A Visit From the Goon Squad*, a national bestseller, won the 2011 National Book Critics Circle Award for Fiction, the 2010 *Los Angeles Times* Book Prize, and was a finalist for the Pen Faulkner Award, as well as a longlist finalist for the UK's Orange Prize. Also a journalist, she writes frequently in the *New York Times Magazine*.

March 2011 | Trade Paperback | Fiction | 352 pp | $14.95 | ISBN 9780307477477
Anchor | readinggroupcenter.com | jenniferegan.com
Also available as: eBook

CONVERSATION STARTERS

1. *A Visit from the Goon Squad* shifts among various perspectives, voices, and time periods, and in one striking chapter (pp. 234–309), departs from conventional narrative entirely. What does the mixture of voices and narrative forms convey about the nature of experience and the creation of memories? Why has Egan arranged the stories out of chronological sequence?

2. In "A to B" Bosco unintentionally coins the phrase "Time's a goon" (p. 127), used again by Bennie in "Pure Language" (p. 332). What does Bosco mean? What does Bennie mean? What does the author mean?

3. "Found Objects" and "The Gold Cure" include accounts of Sasha's and Bennie's therapy sessions. Sasha picks and chooses what she shares: "She did this for Coz's protection and her own—they were writing a story of redemption, of fresh beginnings and second chances" (pp. 8–9). Bennie tries to adhere to a list of no-no's his shrink has supplied (p. 24). What do the tone and the content of these sections suggest about the purpose and value of therapy?

4. Sasha's troubled background comes to light in "Good-bye, My Love" (pp. 208–33). Do Ted's recollections of her childhood explain Sasha's behavior? To what extent is Sasha's "catalog of woes" (p. 213) representative of her generation as a whole? How do Ted's feelings about his career and wife color his reactions to Sasha? What does the flash-forward to "another day more than twenty years after this one" (p. 233) imply about the transitory moments in our lives?

5. The chapters in this book can be read as stand-alone stories. How does this affect the reader's engagement with individual characters and the events in their lives? Which characters or stories did you find the most compelling? By the end, does everything fall into place to form a satisfying storyline?

6. Read the quotation from Proust that Egan uses as an epigraph (p. ix). How do Proust's observations apply to *A Visit from the Goon Squad*? What impact do changing times and different contexts have on how the characters perceive and present themselves? Are the attitudes and actions of some characters more consistent than others', and if so, why?

7. What does "Pure Language" have to say about authenticity in a technological and digital age? Would you view the response to Bennie, Alex, and Lulu's marketing venture differently if the musician had been someone other than Scotty Hausmann and his slide guitar? Stop/Go (from "The Gold Cure"), for example?

The Weird Sisters

By Eleanor Brown

The Andreas family is one of readers. Their father, a renowned Shakespeare professor who speaks almost entirely in verse, has named his three daughters after famous Shakespearean women. When the sisters return to their childhood home, ostensibly to care for their ailing mother, but really to lick their wounds and bury their secrets, they are horrified to find the others there. See, we love each other. We just don't happen to like each other very much. But the sisters soon discover that everything they've been running from—one another, their small hometown, and themselves— might offer more than they ever expected.

"Even if you don't have a sister, you may feel like you have one after reading this hilarious and utterly winsome novel. Eleanor Brown skillfully ties and then unties the Gordian knot of sisterhood, writing with such knowingness that when the ending came, and the three Andreas sisters—who had slunk home for a rest from themselves only to find to their horror their other two sisters there as well—emerge, I sighed the guilty sigh of pleasure and yes, of recognition."—**Sarah Blake, best-selling author of** *The Postmistress*

"At once hilarious, thought-provoking and poignant, this sparkling and devourable debut explores the roles that we play with our siblings, whether we want to or not. The Weird Sisters is a tale of the complex family ties that threaten to pull us apart, but sometimes draw us together instead."
—**J. Courtney Sullivan, best-selling author of** *Commencement*

ABOUT THE AUTHOR: **Eleanor Brown**'s writing has been published in anthologies, magazines, and journals. She holds an M.A. in Literature. Born and raised in the Washington, D.C. area, Eleanor lives in Colorado.

February 2012 | Trade Paperback | Fiction | 368 pp | $15.00 | ISBN 9780425244142
Berkley | penguin.com | eleanorbrown.com
Also available as: eBook and Audiobook

CONVERSATION STARTERS

1. The narration is omniscient first person plural ("we" rather than "I"). Why do you think the author chose to write the novel in this way? Did you like it?

2. Which sister is your favorite? Why? Which sister do you most identify with? Are they the same character?

3. Do you have any siblings? If so, in what way is your relationship with them similar to the relationship among the Andreas sisters? In what way is it different?

4. Each of the sisters has a feeling of failure about where she is in her life and an uncertainty about her position as a grown-up. Are there certain markers that make you an adult, and if so, what are they?

5. In what ways are the sisters' problems of their own making? Does this make them more or less sympathetic?

6. The narrator says that God was always there if the family needed him, "kind of like an extra tube of toothpaste under the sink." Is that true, or does the family's religion have a larger effect on the sisters than they claim? How does your own family's faith, or lack thereof, influence you?

7. How does the Andreas family deal with the mother's illness? How would your family have coped differently?

8. The sisters say that "We have always wondered why there is not more research done on the children of happy marriages." How does their parents' love story affect the sisters? How did your own parents' relationship affect you?

9. What do you think of the sisters' father, James? Is he a good parent? What about their mother?

10. Why do you think the mother is never given a name?

11. The narrators' mother admits that she ended up with the girls' father because she was scared to venture out into the world. Yet she doesn't seem to have any regrets. Do you think there are people who are just not meant to leave home or their comfort zone?

12. Bean and Cordy initially want to leave Barnwell behind, yet they remain, while Rose is the one off living in Europe. Do you think people sometimes become constrained by childhood perceptions of themselves and how their lives will be? How is your own life different from the way you thought it would turn out?

13. When you first saw the title, *The Weird Sisters*, what did you think the book would be about? What do you think the title really means?

Where Lilacs Still Bloom

By Jane Kirkpatrick

German immigrant and farm wife Hulda Klager possesses only an eighth-grade education—and a burning desire to create something beautiful. What begins as a hobby to create an easy-peeling apple for her pies becomes Hulda's driving purpose: a time-consuming interest in plant hybridization that puts her at odds with family and community, as she challenges the early twentieth-century expectations for a simple housewife.

Through the years, seasonal floods continually threaten to erase her Woodland, Washington garden and a series of family tragedies cause even Hulda to question her focus. In a time of practicality, can one person's simple gifts of beauty make a difference?

Based on the life of Hulda Klager, *Where Lilacs Still Bloom* is a story of triumph over an impossible dream and the power of a generous heart.

"Jane Kirkpatrick's attention to detail and ability to craft living, breathing characters immerses the reader into her story world. I come away entranced, enlightened, and enriched after losing myself in one of her novels."
—**Kim Vogel Sawyer, best-selling author of *My Heart Remembers***

ABOUT THE AUTHOR: After 26 years living on Starvation Lane on a remote ranch in Oregon, **Jane Kirkpatrick** and her husband, Jerry, moved back to Bend, Oregon where they'd lived years before. Two dogs and a formerly outdoor cat made the transition well as they begin a new life next to a lily pond instead of the John Day River. *Where Lilacs Still Bloom* is Jane's twenty-second book, her nineteenth novel. She has two lilacs from Hulda Klager's garden.

April 2012 | Trade Paperback | Fiction | 400 pp | $14 .99 | ISBN 9781400074303
WaterBrook Multnomah | waterbrookmultnomah.com | jkbooks.com
Also available as: eBook

CONVERSATION STARTERS

1. What was Hulda Klager's first love? Family? Flowers? Faith? The challenges of cross-breeding? Hulda's father urges her to be faithful to her gift. Did Hulda have a gift or a calling or were her interests and abilities merely passions that she pursued?

2. Hulda comments on the consequences of progress: The electric lighting at the exposition that faded the stars; her objection to indoor plumbing; the impact of steamships docking and ruining the river banks. Yet she sent her children away to pursue their education, celebrated the work of Luther Burbank making changes in food production, worked to have a crisper, bigger apple and 254 individual varieties of lilacs. How do you account for these contradictions in Hulda's character? Did they make her more human or more difficult to understand?

3. Suffering and its consequences and causes was a theme in this book. How did Hulda come to terms with the losses her family endured? Do you think that suffering can be a consequence of pursuing a dream? What role did Hulda's garden play in helping her deal with life's trials?

4. Do you agree with Hulda when she tells her sister: "Beauty matters . . . God gave us flowers for a reason I think so we'd pay attention to the details of creation and remember to trust him in all things big or little no matter what the challenge. Flowers remind us to put away fear, to stop our rushing and running and worrying about this and that and for a moment have a piece of paradise right here on earth."

5. What role did the characters of Jasmine, Nelia, Ruth, Shelly and Cornelia play in this story? Could Hulda's story have been told without them?

6. Where did Hulda draw her strength from to keep going after the deaths of so many in her life? After the flood? Where do you draw your strength from? Are there ways Hulda (and you) enhanced those tools do better face an uncertain future?

7. Dr. Karl Menninger once wrote that the single most important indicator of a person's mental health was generosity. Who was generous in this story? How did generosity bring healing to people of Hulda's world?

8. Did Hulda pay a price for her passion? Would she say that the price was worth it? Do you think it was? Why or why not.

The Widower's Tale

By Julia Glass

Seventy-year-old Percy Darling is settling happily into retirement: reading novels, watching old movies, and swimming naked in his pond. But his routines are disrupted when he is persuaded to let a locally beloved preschool take over his barn. As Percy sees his rural refuge overrun by children, parents, and teachers, he must reexamine the solitary life he has made in the three decades since the sudden death of his wife. With equal parts affection and humor, Julia Glass spins a captivating tale about a man who can no longer remain aloof from his community, his two grown daughters, or—to his great shock—the precarious joy of falling in love.

"Marvelous. . . . A delicate, nuanced, socially conscious story of one family's near-destruction, and how a slew of seemingly bad moves reconnects it." —**USA Today**

"An enchanting story of familial bonds and late-life romance. Expect to be infatuated with Glass's protagonist . . . he of generous soul, dry wit, and courtly manners." —**O, The Oprah Magazine**

"This energized, good-humored novel . . . approaches the ties of kinship with the same joyfully disruptive spirit that animated [Glass's] previous books. . . . Satisfyingly cleareyed and compassionate." —**The New York Times Book Review**

ABOUT THE AUTHOR: **Julia Glass** is the author of *Three Junes*, winner of the 2002 National Book Award for Fiction; *The Whole World Over*; and *I See You Everywhere*, winner of the 2009 Binghamton University John Gardner Book Award. She has received fellowships from the National Endowment for the Arts, the New York Foundation for the Arts, and the Radcliffe Institute for Advanced Study. Her short fiction has won several prizes, and her personal essays have been widely anthologized. She lives in Massachusetts with her family.

July 2011 | Trade Paperback | Fiction | 480 pp | $15.00 | ISBN 9780307456106
Anchor | readinggroupcenter.com
Also available as: eBook and Audiobook

CONVERSATION STARTERS

1. From the stories that the characters remember and tell, what kind of mother (and wife) was Poppy Darling? How would you explain the very different kinds of mothers her two daughters, Trudy and Clover, have become? Discuss the choices these two women have made and how they affect their relationships with their children. And how about Sarah? What kind of mother is she? Does being a mother define any or all of these women?

2. By the end of the novel, how has Percy changed/evolved?

3. Why do you think Percy chose to avoid romantic or sexual involvement for so many years after Poppy's death? Is it habit and routine, nostalgia and commitment to his wife, or guilt over her death; or a combination of all three? Why do you think he falls so suddenly for Sarah after all that time alone? Why now?

4. What do you think of the allusion in this book's title to Chaucer's *Canterbury Tales*?

5. What about Percy's relationship with Clover? What do you think about his "sacrifice" of the barn to help her out? Is it entirely altruistic? What are the unintended consequences to their love for each other? Why does Clover resent her father and betray both him and her nephew, Robert, at the end of the novel?

6. What do you think of Ira and his relationship with Anthony? How have Ira's fears influenced his relationships in general? How do you imagine the crisis at the end of the book has changed him, if at all?

7. "'Daughters.' This word meant everything to me in that moment: sun, moon, stars, blood, water (oh curse the water!), meat, potatoes, wine, shoes, books, the floor beneath my feet, the roof over my head" (p. 125). Compare and contrast Percy's two daughters.

8. While visiting a museum, Percy's friend Norval asks, "So what sort of landscape are you?" Percy replies, "A field. Overgrown and weedy." Norval then suggests, "Or a very large, gnarled tree" (pp. 322–323). How would you describe Percy? How about yourself; what sort of landscape are you?

9. How is *The Widower's Tale* both a tale of our time and a story specific to its place, to New England?

Your Presence is Requested At Suvanto
By Maile Chapman

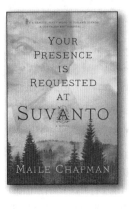

In a remote, piney wood in Finland stands a convalescent hospital called Suvanto, a curving concrete example of austere Scandinavian design. It is the 1920s, and the patients, all women, seek relief from ailments real and imagined. On the lower floors are the stoic Finnish women; on the upper floors are foreign women of privilege—the "uppatients." They are tended to by head nurse Sunny Taylor, an American who has fled an ill-starred life only to retreat behind a mask of crisp professionalism. On a late-summer day a new patient arrives on Sunny's ward—a faded, irascible former ballroom-dance instructor named Julia Dey. Sunny takes it upon herself to pierce the mystery of Julia's reserve. Soon, Julia's difficulty and tightly coiled anger place her at the center of the ward's tangled emotional life. As summer turns to fall, and fall to a long, dark winter, the patients hear rumors about changes being implemented at Suvanto by an American obstetrician, Dr. Peter Weber, who is experimenting with a new surgical stitch. Their familiar routine threatened, the women are not happy, and the story's escalating menace builds to a terrifying conclusion.

"Maile Chapman is one of my favorite writers and in Your Presence Is Requested at Suvanto *she has given us an eerie gift of a novel. It is a superb hallucinatory piercing, an ominous dispatch from that Gothic frontier of the Female Body."* —**Junot Díaz**

"Chapman has written more than a beautifully observed and utterly convincing first novel: she has written something of unfakeable importance." —**Tom Bissel**

About the Author: **Maile Chapman**'s stories have appeared in *A Public Space,* the *Literary Review,* the *Mississippi Review,* and *Post Road.* She earned her MFA from Syracuse University and has been a fellow at the Dorothy and Lewis B. Cullman Center for Scholars and Writers in the New York Public Library.

June 2011 | Trade Paperback | Fiction | 280 pp | $15.00 | ISBN 9781555975876
Graywolf Press | graywolfpress.org | mailechapman.com
Also available as: eBook

CONVERSATION STARTERS

1. What role does cultural alienation play in the novel? Why did Sunny choose such a remote and foreign place to live and work? Was she prepared for the challenges?

2. *Your Presence Is Requested at Suvanto* employs two distinct points of view, the first person plural and the third person omniscient. What is the purpose of the choral voice? What is the effect of shifting from one point of view to the other?

3. Who is speaking in passages such as the following on page 99: "[Sunny's] work is nearly meaningless, and life is nothing but a search for meaning, yes? Isn't that right?" How would you describe this tone, and how does that affect your interpretation of events?

4. How do the changing seasons and weather affect the development of the narrative? What role does landscape play in the book generally?

5. Chapman often describes the aging body with unflinching precision. How are we meant to react to the degradation and failings of the body? What do you think the author is saying about her characters' attitude toward their bodies?

6. Before she came to Suvanto, Sunny was caring for her ailing mother. In other words, she is often in the position of attending to others without addressing the reality of her own needs. What do you think Sunny needs? Is she capable of taking care of herself?

7. Julia Dey, the ex-ballroom dancer from Denmark, instigates much of the book's tension. She is a menace and pest, but she can also be funny and charismatic. Did you sympathize with Julia's predicament? Given all the trouble she causes, why are the patients so outraged by her eventual death?

8. According to Pearl's husband William Weber on page 212, she has "actively chosen to make herself ill. She is, as she has always tried to convince him, not like other women." Is this is a fair conclusion? Are all of the up-patients simply neurotic? If not, what is wrong with them?

9. Despite the apparent order and efficiency and high level of professionalism at the hospital, we discover that it is as much an economic system as a medical facility. Care is not necessarily distributed equitably among those who need it on the lower floors. Does *Your Presence Is Requested at Suvanto* have anything to say about contemporary healthcare issues?

10. Although some reviewers called the novel a "thriller," it does not really rely on cliffhangers or plot twists for momentum. How does Chapman ratchet up the tension and create an atmosphere of anxious menace?

What will happen when the truth is e x p o s e d?

Liz is confident that she and Kate will be best friends forever. But then, Kate makes a startling accusation that changes everything Liz believed was true about photography, family, friendship, and even herself.

Use these discussion questions to talk about *Exposed* in your book club!

- Liz doesn't know who to believe—her brother or her best friend. Who do you believe?

- Kate says she is glad she came forward, despite everything that follows. Why do you think she feels this way?

- Why do you think the author chose to write this story in verse? How do you think the story would have been different if it were in prose? Do you think verse was the right choice for this story?

RHCB   Delacorte Press

Read & Discuss.

HOW DO YOU KNOW IF YOU'RE TO BLAME?

After a bullied classmate commits suicide, Kana is sent to her grandparents' for the summer. Kana wasn't the bully, but she didn't do anything to stop what happened, either. As Kana comes to terms with the role she played, news from home will send her world spinning out of orbit.

Use these discussion questions to talk about *Orchards* in your book club!

- School bullying seems to be universal. Do you believe a passive bystander can be as guilty as the person who does the overt bullying?

- Why do you think author Holly Thompson chose to write from the point of view of Kana, a girl who contributed to the bullying rather than the girl being bullied? And how is Ruth present as a character throughout the novel?

- *Orchards* is a novel in verse. Do you feel it would have the same impact, or be different, if written in prose?

RandomBuzzers.com

The Gripping New Novel from
jenny downham

When Mikey's sister claims a boy assaulted her, his world begins to fall apart.

When Ellie's brother is charged with the offense, her world begins to unravel.

When Mikey and Ellie meet, two worlds collide.

READ & DISCUSS

- Both Karyn and Ellie are afraid of going to court. Debate whether they have conquered their fears by the end of the novel.

- Compare and contrast Ellie's relationship with Tom to Karyn's relationship with Mikey. How do Ellie and Tom restore their relationship at the end of the novel, in spite of their father?

- At the end of the novel, Mikey says, "Maybe we can grab something good out of this while we can." (p. 409) What good has come out of this entire situation? Discuss whether the novel is Ellie and Mikey's story or Karyn and Tom's story.

ANOTHER GREAT READ!

Before I Die

Read an excerpt at RandomBuzzers.com

extremely witty conversation with southern authors
most excellent recommendations for reading
clever & refined musings of booksellers & writers
engaging & amusing author readings
illuminating excerpts from great southern books
and other such items as are of interest to
her ladyship, the editor

Lady Banks' Commonplace Book

front porch literary gossip
from your favorite southern bookshops

subscribe at ladybankscommonplacebook.com

GUIDELINES FOR
Lively Book Discussions

Respect space—Avoid "crosstalk" or talking over others.

Allow space—Some of us are more outgoing and others more reserved. If you've had a chance to talk, allow others time to offer their thoughts as well.

Be open—Keep an open mind, learn from others, and acknowledge there are differences in opinion. That's what makes it interesting!

Offer new thoughts—Try not to repeat what others have said, but offer a new perspective.

Stay on the topic—Contribute to the flow of conversation by holding your comments to the topic of the book, keeping any personal references to an appropriate minimum.

Come find, friend, and follow us

On the web: **ReadingGroupChoices.com**

On our blog: **OntheBookcase.com**

On Facebook: **Reading Group Choices Fan Page**

On Twitter: **@ReadingGChoices**

READING GROUP Choices

We wish to thank the authors, agents, publicists, librarians, booksellers, and our publishing colleagues who have continued to support this publication by calling to our attention some quality books for group discussion, and the publishers and friends who have helped to underwrite this edition.

Algonquin Books

Anchor

Atria

Ballantine Books

Berkley

Broadway Books

Da Capo Lifelong Books

Dafina

David Fickling Books

Graywolf Press

Grove Atlantic

Harper Paperbacks

Harper Perennial

Houghton Mifflin Harcourt

Hyperion Books

Kensington Books

Mariner Books

New American Library

Other Press

Penguin Books

Picador

PublicAffairs

Random House

Random House Children's Books

Random House Trade Paperbacks

Riverhead Books

Rodale

Southern Independent Booksellers Alliance

Vintage Books

Voice

Washington Square Press

WaterBrook Multnomah

William Morrow

William Morrow Paperbacks

W.W. Norton & Company

Reading Group Choices' goal is to join with publishers, bookstores, libraries, trade associations, and authors to develop resources to enhance the shared reading group experience.

Reading Group Choices is distributed annually to bookstores, libraries, and directly to book groups. Titles from previous issues are posted on the **www.ReadingGroupChoices.com** website. Books presented here have been recommended by book group members, librarians, booksellers, literary agents, publicists, authors, and publishers. All submissions are then reviewed to ensure the discussibility of each title. Once a title is approved for inclusion by the Advisory Board (see below), publishers are asked to underwrite production costs, so that copies of *Reading Group Choices* can be distributed for a minimal charge.

For additional copies, please call your local library or bookstore, or contact us by phone or email as shown below. Quantities are limited. For more information, please visit our website at **www.ReadingGroupChoices.com**

Toll-free: 1-866-643-6883 • info@ReadingGroupChoices.com

READING GROUP CHOICES' ADVISORY BOARD

Donna Paz Kaufman founded the bookstore training and consulting group of Paz & Associates in 1992, with the objective of creating products and services to help independent bookstores and public libraries remain viable in today's market. A few years later, she met and married **Mark Kaufman**, whose background included project management, marketing communications, and human resources. Together, they launched **Reading Group Choices** in 1994 to bring publishers, booksellers, libraries, and readers closer together. They sold **Reading Group Choices** to Barbara and Charlie Mead in May 2005. They now offer training and education for new and prospective booksellers, architectural design services for bookstores and libraries, marketing support, and a training library for professional and staff development on a wide variety of topics. To learn more about Paz & Associates, visit www.PazBookBiz.com.

John Mutter is editor-in-chief of *Shelf Awareness*, the daily e-mail newsletter focusing on books, media about books, retailing and related issues to help booksellers, librarians and others do their jobs more effectively. Before he and his business partner, Jenn Risko, founded the company in May 2005, he was executive editor of bookselling at *Publishers Weekly*. He has covered book industry issues for 25 years and written for a variety of publications, including *The Bookseller* in the U.K.; *Australian Bookseller & Publisher*; *Boersenblatt*, the German book trade magazine; and *College Store Magazine* in the U.S. For more information about *Shelf Awareness*, go to its Web site, www.shelf-awareness.com.

Mark Nichols was an independent bookseller in various locations from Maine to Connecticut from 1976 through 1993. After seven years in a variety of positions with major publishers in New York and San Francisco, he joined the American Booksellers Association in 2000, and currently serves as Senior Director, Publisher Initiatives. He is on the Board of James Patterson's ReadKiddoRead.com, and has edited two volumes with Newmarket Press—*Book Sense Best Books* (2004) and *Book Sense Best Children's Book*s (2005).

Nancy Olson has owned and operated Quail Ridge Books & Music in Raleigh, NC, since 1984, which has grown from 1,200 sq. ft. to 9,000+ sq. ft and sales of $3.2 million. The bookstore won three major awards in 2001: *Publishers Weekly* Bookseller of the Year, Charles Haslam Award for Excellence in Bookselling; Pannell Award for Excellence in Children's Bookselling. It was voted "Best in the Triangle" in the *Independent Weekly* and *Metro Magazine*.

Jill A. Tardiff is publishing industry consultant and project manager working under her banner company Bamboo River Associates. She is also advertising manager for such print and online publications as *Parabola—Tradition, Myth, and the Search for Meaning*, as well as contributing editor at *Publishers Weekly*. Jill is the past president of the Women's National Book Association (WNBA) and WNBA-New York City chapter, 2004–2006 and 2000–2005, respectively. She is currently WNBA's National Reading Group Month Committee Chair and Coordinator and its United Nations Department of Public Information NGO Chief Representative. She is currently working on several book proposals on modern-day pilgrimage.

Book Group Resources

About reading groups and book clubs

- **ReadingGroupChoices.com**—Over 1000 guides available plus giveaways and fun and interactive materials for reading groups.

- **bookgroupexpo.com**—Come to book group expo and celebrate.

- **Book-Clubs-Resource.com**—A guide to book clubs and reading groups with a collection of links and information for readers, including information about saving with discount book clubs.

- **BookClubCookbook.com**—Recipes and food for thought from your book club's favorite books and authors

- **bookclubgirl.com**—Dedicated to sharing great books, news, and tips with book club girls everywhere

- **bookgroupbuzz.booklistonline.com**—Book group tips, reading lists, & lively talk of literary news from the experts at Booklist Online

- **NationalReadingGroupMonth.org**—Celebrating the joy of shared reading

- **LiteraryAffairs.net**—Book club picks and author events from one of the leading book club facilitators in the country

About Books

- **ShelfAwareness.com**—A free e-mail newsletter dedicated to helping the people in stores, in libraries and on the Web buy, sell, and lend books most wisely.

- **GenerousBooks.com**—A community for those who love books and love to discuss them

- **BookMuse.com**— Commentary, author bios, and suggestions for further reading

- **BookBrowse.com**—Book reviews, excerpts, and author interviews

- **BookSpot.com**—Help in your search for the best book-related content on the Web

- **Publisher Websites**—Find additional topics for discussion, special offers for book groups, and other titles of interest.

Algonquin Books — **algonquin.com**

Anchor — **readinggroupcenter.com**

Atria — **imprints.simonandschuster.biz/atria**

Ballantine Books — **atrandom.com**

Berkley — **penguin.com**

Broadway Books — **crownpublishing.com**

Da Capo Lifelong Books — **perseusbooksgroup.com**

Dafina — **kensingtonbooks.com**

David Fickling Books — **RandomBuzzers.com**

Graywolf Press — **graywolfpress.org**

Grove Atlantic — **groveatlantic.com**

Harper Paperbacks — **harpercollins.com**

Harper Perennial — **harperperennial.com**

Houghton Mifflin Harcourt — **houghtonmifflinbooks.com**

Hyperion Books — **hyperionbooks.com**

Kensington Books — **kensingtonbooks.com**

Mariner Books — **marinerbooks.com**

New American Library — **penguin.com**

Other Press — **otherpress.com**

Penguin Books — **penguin.com**

Picador — **picadorusa.com**

PublicAffairs — **publicaffairsbooks.com**

Random House — **randomhouse.com**

Random House Children's Books — **kidsatrandom.com**

Random House Trade Paperbacks — **atrandom.com**

Riverhead Books — **penguin.com**

Rodale — **rodale.com**

Vintage Books — **readinggroupcenter.com**

Voice — **everywomansvoice.com**

Washington Square Press — **imprints.simonandschuster.biz/atria**

William Morrow — **williammorrow.com**

William Morrow Paperbacks — **williammorrow.com**

W.W. Norton & Company — **wwnorton.com**